I0769742

For those who are still discovering themselves,
cannot come out publicly,
or are struggling with religious trauma.
I hope this story brings you peace and understanding.
You are not faulty. You are not confused. You are not *wrong*.
The fall from grace is scary, but oh so worth it.

Contents

This book contains themes that may be disturbing to some readers, including experimentation with light bondage, physical assault/torture, blood, and self-mutilation (removal of non-human appendages).

1

S HADES OF PURPLE, ORANGE, and pink took their places in the sky. Fallon sat on a white stool, admiring her own work with her head perched in her hands, gazing out at the same sky she watched every night. A loaf was resting on the counter, almost ready to go into the oven; it was just missing the finishing touch.

Fallon smiled when a knock sounded at her door. "Come in!"

Victoria managed to get the door open and slammed it shut with her hip, her hands full with a basket of various flowers and herbs. "Am I too late?"

Fallon shook her head. "Nope, you're perfect." She lightly tapped Victoria's nose and took the basket from her hands. "You go ahead, I'll place these."

Without another word, Victoria plopped down on the stool Fallon previously occupied. After looking through the flowers, Fallon decided on a few blue and purple ones; Victoria's favorite colors. Delicately, Fallon laid them out on the sourdough loaf and flattened the petals into the dough.

A gust of scorching air waved onto Fallon's face and blew through the feathers of her wings as she opened the oven, and slid the brightly decorated dough inside.

Victoria waved her over excitedly and scooched their stools so close that the feathers on their wings mingled. She sighed. "Isn't it beautiful?"

Fallon chuckled softly and handed her a mug of hot chamomile tea. Their fingers brushed, sending the usual zap through Fallon. "It always is. Especially pretty tonight, I think." She stared at Victoria, who hadn't taken her eyes off the sunset. They watched it together *every* night.

The two sat in awe as the sun sank lower and lower into the clouds without conversation, always content in the other's company. When the light began to dim, they retired to the couch to wait for the bread to bake.

"Another great day." Victoria took a sip from her mug. "We outdid ourselves with that one."

"We're great at our job, what can we say?" Fallon raised her own mug slightly in a toast to their hard work. "Those clouds won't paint themselves."

"I didn't say anything earlier, but I thought you used too much orange." Fallon gasped, and Victoria rubbed her forearm soothingly, her touch lingering. "I am glad to be mistaken."

Fallon's eyes grew wide, almost choking on her tea. "Did you just admit to being wrong?"

"And I'll never do it again." Victoria exhaled as her chin kicked to the side at the fact.

Laughter filled Fallon's living room as they recounted their day. A fellow cloud painter, Orson, had tripped on a cirrus cloud. He barely avoided falling over, his wings large enough to keep him balanced. Of course, it helped that Fallon sent a small gust of wind to keep him upright.

"Do you think he noticed that you helped him?"

Fallon shrugged. "If he did, he didn't say anything. He's too proud." Many of them were. Asking for help and admitting fault were things every angel in Heaven would pray for guidance about.

Victoria's brows shot up. "You're telling me! He'd better be at service on Wednesday." She shook her head and took a deep breath, her eyes falling shut. When they popped open, they locked onto Fallon. "That smells *amazing*." Victoria jumped up and ran to the oven, then sat cross-legged on the ground in front of it.

Fallon looked over her wing into the kitchen and laughed. "It's not finished yet, Vic. A few more minutes, and then it needs to sit."

Victoria groaned as her head fell forward, the part in her hair shifting. Fallon's fingers twitched as she thought about fixing it. "But I want it nooww. You make the best sourdough," she complained.

"You poor thing. How would you survive without me?" Fallon teased and stuck out her tongue. Victoria looked unenthused. "It'll be finished soon, dove. Be patient."

Victoria rolled her eyes and huffed dramatically. "Fine, I guess I can fill my time with something else." Her long, warm-brown hair fell over her shoulder as she scrambled to her feet and started sorting through the remaining flowers she had brought. Stems and petals of every size fell onto the light wood countertop, mixing with the remnants of flour from Fallon's baking.

Fallon peeled herself from her mauve-pink couch and leaned against the white marble counter to silently watch.

Victoria had picked out every pink and yellow flower from the basket and laid them next to each other. One by one, she added them to a bundle in her hand. Peonies, Azaleas, and Poppies dominated the mix.

Fallon's eyes never left Victoria, entranced. "What are you doing over there?"

Victoria's eyes sliced to the side, squinting. "*Be patient,*" she mimicked.

So, she was patient.

The two sat in the warm glow of lit candles as Victoria plucked smaller buds from the counter, and situated them between the bigger flowers. With a fist full of stems, she looked around the kitchen for something to tie them with, settling for a piece of light blue ribbon peeking out of a book.

"Hey! That was a bookmark," Fallon groaned as she rubbed the outside of her arm with her palm.

Victoria giggled. "I'll give you a million more bookmarks, Lonnie. I need this one," she explained as she wrapped the ribbon around the bundle of pink sunshine before holding it out toward Fallon, whose brow furrowed.

"What's this?" She brought the bouquet to her face and breathed deeply, taking in the freshness.

"It's for you. Just a little something to say thank you for always hosting."

Fallon scoffed. "I'd hardly call it hosting, it's only ever just the two of us."

Victoria shrugged. "Those are the only two people I care about." She washed the flour off her hands and started digging through the cabinets without realizing Fallon's flushed cheeks.

Giggling, Fallon asked, "What are you doing *now*?"

"Looking for a vase," Victoria answered matter-of-factly.

"There's one un—,"

"Found it!" She filled the vase at the sink, and centered it on the kitchen island with Fallon's cutting board.

Fallon smiled at her and shook her head as she placed the flowers in the vase. She crossed her arms and took a step back. "They're beautiful, thank you."

Victoria waved her hand. "It's nothing you don't deserve," she murmured as she rested her head on Fallon's shoulder. "Not to be dramatic, but I may die if I don't eat that bread soon."

A harsh laugh left Fallon. "As long as you're not being dramatic."

"It's not my fault you decided to wait till the last minute to bake it."

Fallon looked at her with pinched brows. "Was I not waiting for *you* to bring the flowers?"

Victoria's tongue poked the inside of her cheek as she stared at Fallon. "Right, well, who can say who was at fault, really?" Her cheeks turned pink as she twirled a strand of hair around her finger.

Fallon's eyes were drawn to the movement. "Let me see your nails," she prompted as she held out a hand.

Victoria flared her fingers in front of Fallon and wiggled them. "See them?" She squealed when Fallon grabbed her hand out of the air and pulled it close.

"This color is adorable! You'll have to paint mine this time."

Victoria smiled softly. "How much time do we have?"

Groaning, Fallon stretched to look at the oven and peek at the baking bread. "I'd say maybe five more minutes. Is that enough time?"

Swift as the wind, Victoria jumped up and headed for the door. "I'll make it enough time!" she shouted right before the door slammed shut. As soon as it did, Fallon shot up and stared out the window, watching her dove run home to grab the polish.

She let out a deep, heavy breath and smiled to herself. No one made her happy like Victoria.

As if summoned by the thought, her face reappeared as she ran back across the short distance between their homes.

They had the two closest homes in Heaven, insisting a street of distance would be too far apart.

Victoria ushered Fallon back onto her blue gingham cushioned stool and positioned her hand to be painted. With exercised precision, she swept the brush down each nail, avoiding skin and cuticle. She held each finger as if they were so delicate, they might break. After a few minutes, she lowered her face and lightly blew to help the polish dry faster. Her eyes lingered on Fallon's arm as goosebumps appeared, the hairs standing.

"Okay, keep that hand still while I do the other one," Victoria instructed.

"Yes, ma'am," Fallon said with a playful salute.

Victoria groaned. "I *just* told you not to move, Lonnie."

"Right, sorry."

She finished Fallon's nails and fanned them with her hand before twisting the polish closed and looking over her work.

"Cute! Now we're matching," Victoria cheered as she wiggled her fingers at Fallon again.

"I don't think I thought this through. I can't put my mitts on with wet nails..." She looked back and forth between her freshly painted claws and the pale pink oven mitts on the counter.

Victoria let out a playful huff. "You truly would be lost without me," she joked as she pulled the mitts onto her hands and opened the oven.

"I didn't say it was ready," Fallon laughed.

The oven door squeaked as Victoria closed it with her foot before placing the pan on the stove. "I'm making the executive decision that it's finished. I hope you understand," she explained, her eyes closed while she inhaled. Victoria moaned, her mouth watering. "Ugh, I love you. You're too good to me."

Her heart skipped. "I made bread, Vic," Fallon said in hushed disbelief.

Victoria's head snapped to look at her. "And? Let me be grateful. Go sit down and pick our movie, I'll cut this up and bring some to you."

Fallon placed a peck on Victoria's head as she walked by her to the couch. "You're the best," she cheered as she pulled a fuzzy blanket over her.

Victoria smiled and shook her head softly to herself. "Don't say I never do anything for you."

"I quite value my life, thank you," Fallon joked as she slowly flipped through the discs in their movie collection, considering every option.

The couch sank as Victoria sat with a plate of sliced bread in her hand. "Can we watch *Get the Girl*?"

Fallon's hands froze as she slowly looked over at Victoria. "We watched that four days ago."

Victoria didn't blink. "What's your point?"

Fallon's pale blonde hair fell over her shoulder as she got up from the couch and set up the movie. "I can't say no to you, can I?"

"You'd be wise not to."

Shadows from the movie screen cast onto the walls, the hall filled with framed photos of laughing girls and summer days spent in the garden. Polaroid photos arranged in collages surrounded by pressed flowers hung above the couch over their heads, each one a favorite memory surrounded by the florals they acquired on their adventures. As credits rolled on the screen, Fallon yawned quietly. Victoria fell asleep about halfway through the movie, like always, and Fallon decided to let her rest. The two shared a blanket, huddling together for warmth. Victoria had told Fallon countless times that she kept her house too cold, but Fallon liked it that way—all the baking made it warm inside.

And they got to share blankets.

Fallon tried to shift her arm out from underneath Victoria's without waking her, and froze when she let out a soft hum. She was going to have to stay put, then; she refused to wake her. Fallon stayed there on the couch, holding a softly snoring Victoria until she finally drifted to sleep herself.

2

FALLON STOLE A GLIMPSE of Victoria in the middle of the silence before final prayer. Victoria was already peeking at her. She barely choked back a laugh in time, able to hide it with a sniffle. The angel in the pew in front of them turned her head and eyed them down, telling them to be quiet with just the intensity of her stare. Victoria quietly apologized and shut her eyes again in an attempt to be respectful.

Fallon poked her leg, crumbling the frail restraint Victoria was holding onto. The two of them snorted under their breath right as the seraph leading the service told them to stand for prayer. Every angel in the sanctuary reached for each other's hands and bowed their heads. Fallon looked over at Victoria, who smiled sweetly back at her.

It was Fallon's favorite part of service.

She gingerly reached for Victoria's hand, their fingers interlocking before they finally bowed their heads.

"Dear Heavenly Father, quit vivit et regnat in saecula saeculorum,

We thank you for allowing us into your home. We thank you for giving us the opportunity to work for you and with you for eternity, and for creating the perfect sanctuary both in and outside these walls. We will take these gifts and put them to good use.

Amen."

Rows of angels replied, "Amen," and were dismissed.

Fallon and Victoria went to the same place they did after every service: the courtyard. Something about the sunshine and soft grass put Fallon at ease after stressful situations.

Streaks of light flashed in Fallon's vision from squinting so hard. She fiddled with the hat in her hands, rubbing the blue silk ribbon against her thumb.

"If only there was something you could use to keep the sun out of your eyes," Victoria said with a smirk.

"You're *so* funny," Fallon sneered.

"Just put the hat on, Lonnie. It won't do you any good if it's not on your head."

Fallon drew her bottom lip between her teeth and fidgeted with the ribbon again. Victoria's rich brown eyes fell to the silky strand and noticed Fallon's hands slightly trembling.

"Feeling anxious again?"

Fallon nodded sheepishly. "Yeah, a bit. I feel fine, though, don't worry about me."

Victoria tsked. "You know I will anyway. Try that exercise we went through last week. Three things you can see, touch, smell—that whole thing."

Fallon took a steadying breath and nodded again as she closed her eyes to tune into her senses. "I can smell the garlic bread," she said as she placed her hand on her stomach, which made Victoria laugh. "I still smell the communion wine, and...your perfume." When Fallon opened her eyes, Victoria was smiling at her.

"Good. Alright, sight next," she told her as she smoothed her skirt over her legs.

"Clouds."

"*Ha ha*," Victoria joked, and lightly pushed Fallon's shoulder.

"Gingham," Fallon said, looking down at their lavender blanket. Her green eyes shifted to the right. "The white marble columns of the pergola." Then the left. "The serenity pond."

"Perfect. Feel better yet?"

Fallon shrugged. "A little." She finally placed the hat on her head.

"You're not done yet, Fal," she reminded her in a singsong voice.

Fallon groaned, her fingers still on the brim of her wide-brimmed hat. "Straw." She closed her eyes and clenched her hand at her side. "Do I really have to finish this?"

Victoria nodded with raised eyebrows, earning a groan from Fallon.

Her hand unclenched, her fingers splayed on the ground. "Grass." She tilted her head back. "And the Sun. No goosebumps today," she points out as she holds out her arm. "I feel better enough, I suppose."

Victoria placed her hand on Fallon's knee, rubbing her thumb to comfort her. "Proud of you. Now, where were we?" Victoria plucked a single blue flower from the field beneath them and started wrapping the stem around her finger. Once it was coiled, she pulled it off and tied a small piece of twine around the stem to keep it together.

Fallon held out her hand, fingers spread apart. "See if it fits."

One by one, Victoria put the flower ring onto each of Fallon's fingers until it slid all the way onto her fourth one, next to her pinky. "Perfect! My turn."

Fallon looked all around them and settled on a puff of a little pink flower before repeating Victoria's steps. Fallon slid the flower around Victoria's fourth finger, and it fit just as perfectly. "There, now we're matching again."

Their giggling and smiling attracted the attention of other nearby angels who were relaxing after service. Acquaintances, coworkers; the field was crowded, everyone wanting to soak in the Sun. A few of the neighboring loungers exchanged whispers with lingering stares.

Fallon was always the first to notice, and her already fragile smile faded from her face. She cleared her throat and lowered her voice, intent on shooing away any unwanted eyes. She and Victoria often attracted nosey bystanders, judgmental minds who thought they knew more than they did.

It happened every time they went out together.

Victoria never noticed the stares, too concerned with Fallon's change in behavior. "Would you like to go home? We can have our picnic in the backyard if it's too crowded here. I'm getting a little warm, myself," she lied to not make Fallon feel bad about leaving.

"That might be best," Fallon confessed with sad eyes. "I'm sorry, Vic, I don't know what's going on with me today."

Victoria started to place their goods into her basket so Fallon could fold the blanket. "Nonsense. I'd much rather be able to use my own bathroom and be a step away from a couch." She moved Fallon's hair behind her shoulder, her fingers lingering on the soft skin of her shoulder. "Let's go home," she said as she tapped beneath her chin.

After quickly flying home, Fallon flopped onto the couch with a huff and pulled her silky blonde hair over her face like a cage. She went down with such force that she pushed the rug with her foot, taking the coffee table with it.

"You did great today, Fal. It'll get easier," Victoria promised as she sat next to her friend.

"*When?*" She asked, exasperated. She could barely see through her blonde strands, but could feel Victoria's concern. "I'm sorry, dove. We love our courtyard picnics, and now I've ruined one," she muffled through her hair.

Victoria wasn't pleased, but she certainly didn't place any blame on Fallon. "You didn't ruin anything; it's no one's fault." Her finger delicately poked through the wall of silk and pulled it apart. "Why don't you take a bath, hm? Warm water, some smell-good oils, light some candles. It'll be relaxing."

Fallon groaned, feeling dirty despite her skin being completely clean. "I'd rather sit here in my filth and wallow," she croaked as she pulled her hair closed again.

Victoria swatted her on the thigh, trying to snap her out of her fog. "Too bad, that's not allowed."

"Hey!" Fallon laughed. "That stung." It surprised her more than it hurt.

"Get up, or I'll do it again," Victoria threatened her, winding her arm back.

"You wouldn't..." Her eyes turned to slits, her heart fluttering at the idea of her following through.

"I *so* would."

Shrieks echoed through the halls as Victoria tried to force relaxation upon her. Their feet moved quicker than their minds as they bumped into walls and shook the framed photos there.

"Get in the tub, Lon!" Victoria shouted through a giggle.

"You can't make me!"

Victoria chuckled. "Challenge accepted." She snuck off to fill the bath as Fallon hid in the living room. She ducked behind the couch, completely forgetting about the white, feathered wings that reached far above her head.

When the water turned on, Fallon closed her eyes and hoped she wouldn't be found.

But she could never hide from her dove.

With a yell, Fallon was pulled into the hall. Victoria guided her to the bathroom, using her body as a blockade until she shut the bathroom door behind them.

"Let me out of here!" Fallon barely said through her laugh.

Victoria was already reaching for the showerhead on the left wall, aiming it at Fallon. "Don't move, or I'll spray you."

Fallon gasped. "You wouldn't dare," she challenged with her eyes wide.

Victoria shifted, making Fallon flinch, and pointed at the tub.

"I'm not going to waste our time together!" She said as she raised her hands in surrender. "I can bathe later when you're busy."

"Who said you were going to be alone?" Victoria asked with a cocked brow.

Before Fallon could blink, Victoria stepped into the tub and put a hand around her wrist. Fallon took a step to keep from falling, but ended up in the tub despite her efforts. Bubbles flew into the air as warm water soaked through her white dress. Lips parted, she looked at Victoria. She couldn't stop her eyes from trailing down and admiring her friend. Then, she splashed a small tidal wave in her direction.

Victoria's warm brown hair stuck to her face as her jaw fell, and she wiped the bubbly water from her eyes. "You know what? Fair enough."

"This is a new dress, you jerk."

"It looks amazing on you, by the way," she said calmly, like she hadn't chased her friend through the house. "It's water, not molasses. It'll dry, Lon."

Fallon rolled her eyes.

"Now that you're here, you might as well soak."

"I don't like pruning," Fallon huffed as she crossed her arms.

"You don't have to prune, just take some time for yourself. You deserve to take a moment, forced or otherwise, to take some deep breaths and not do anything."

Fallon released an exaggerated breath, bubbles blowing forward onto Victoria's glistening chest.

"Fine."

"Look where you're going!" Fallon warned. The rocks were slippery; she had lost her footing twice already, the hem of her skirt damp from misplaced steps.

Victoria looked back over her shoulder and smiled. "You worry too much! It's fine," she assured her, and leapt to the next stone in the river.

"Would you at least watch your feet? You almost missed that one, dove, don't go splitting anything open."

"You're being dramatic," Victoria complained as she continued down the stones. "I've done this so many times at this point, I don't even need to look." She placed a hand over her eyes and took another step, gracefully moving further down the rocky path.

Fallon's breath hitched as she watched, her hand flying forward to send a helpful gust of wind. She was so focused on making sure Victoria didn't fall that she lost her footing and splashed into the water.

When Victoria whipped her head, she found Fallon knee deep in the chilled water. She tried to stifle her laugh, and failed.

Fallon huffed, a strand of hair blowing up and falling back down on her face. "Great, now my wings are wet."

Victoria's hand flew to her mouth before reaching down toward Fallon. "Need some help?"

Stubborn as always, Fallon tried to push herself up in the running water. The stream broke around her legs, rippling out on either side. The slickness of the rocks beneath her, combined with the weight of dampened wings, forbade her from doing it alone. After two failed attempts, her frustration outbid her pride, and she allowed Victoria to pull her up.

Once righted, Victoria didn't let go. Fingers entwined, she led Fallon step by step over the stones. A particularly long step stretched their arms so far that their fingers nearly separated, but they held firm and continued together.

While they looked for rocks to paint on, they rambled about possible designs.

"I'm trying to think of a flower," Victoria mumbled.

Fallon's hand flew to her chest, feigning surprise. "You? Painting a flower? How unheard of," she teased. "You paint at least one every time."

"Can you blame me? They're beautiful." Her shoulders rise and fall as visions of petals fill her mind.

"They *are* pretty." Her eyes lingered on the joy in her face. "I'm keeping my painting a secret," she said. "You'll love it though, I know it."

"Wait, no!" She flipped a paintbrush around in her hand and poked Fallon's shoulder. "You have to tell me, I told you mine!" she whined.

"Yours is hardly a surprise, dove. Flowers are kind of your thing," she reminds her.

"Fine, secret keeper. Keep your secrets." Victoria pouted, her bottom lip poking out as her eyes grew wide.

"You'll see when I'm finished."

They found a space they deemed suitable to set up their blanket and cups. Victoria thoroughly looked through the bag she brought before dumping it out next to her. "Did you bring any green paint?"

"Vic...You planned on painting a flower and didn't bring green?"

Her forehead creased. "What, like you never forget anything? Not all of us can be perfect angels with flawless memories."

Fallon scoffed. "I am no perfect angel, dove." She shook her head and reached for her tube of green paint. "Here, just don't use it all."

With teasing eyes, Victoria said, "I'll try."

Chattering birds and babbling water filled their ears as they painted, cleaning their brushes with cups of river water. The Sun caused no harm in Heaven; they could bask in the light for hours without worrying about pain or redness.

"Can I see it yet?"

"No, Vic."

"What about now?" she tried.

"Yes, actually."

"Wait, really? I didn't think that would work."

Fallon took a deep breath and turned her rock toward Victoria to reveal a pale blue background with soft clouds in their usual sunset shades, with a single white bird in the center.

"Lon, is that…" She lifted her pointer finger slowly toward the rock.

"Yep." Fallon took her bottom lip between her teeth. "It's my dove," she explained with a shrug.

Victoria's eyes filled with tears as she looked at the palm-sized painting. "Fallon, that's beautiful," she muttered. Her arms flew around Fallon's neck, and they melted into each other. "You make my flower look like child's play," she mumbled against Fallon's skin.

Fallon chuckled and pulled away. "You could never do anything less than wonderful."

"You make me blush," Victoria confessed as she tried to hide her face.

"Don't hide from me now, dove. It's a little late for that, don't you think?" Fallon put her hand on Victoria's shoulder and pushed down lightly to right her posture.

"Good point," she admitted. "I'm ready for lunch. Time to go home?"

They stacked the cups and capped the paints before picking up the corners of the blanket. It acted as a sack, filled with brushes and rocks as they moved back across the water to Fallon's house.

Fallon decided to whip up a snack. When the oven beeped, it cut through the tired silence and startled her. "I got it!" she shouted as she jumped from the couch.

Victoria followed her anyway, even though the hard part was finished. Without thinking, she jumped up and sat on the island, her butt landing on remnants of flour that always seemed to be on Fallon's kitchen counter. She closed her eyes and took an exaggerated breath. "I want a candle that smells like your cookies."

"Don't we have enough hobbies? Now we need to take up candle making?" Fallon placed the tray of cookies on the stove before taking off her mitts and putting them next to Victoria. A small cloud of flour flew into the air around them from the force. "Vic, I think you're sitting on flour…"

"You're joking!" She jumped down and tried to look at her own backside, shifting her skirt in the process. Fallon already had a rag in her hand and held it out to Victoria. She swiped and patted the flour, but she could only reach so far. "Would you mind? I can't see it all." She handed the rag back to Fallon and turned to face the counter.

Fallon's knuckles turned white from her vice grip on the rag, her mouth a thin line. She nodded to herself and swiped repeatedly down Victoria's behind and legs until the flour was gone. Victoria turned abruptly, and the two stood face-to-face in Fallon's kitchen.

"Thank you."

"Any time, dove."

3

"**O**H SHOOT, I'M GOING to be late!"

Fallon scrambled to get dressed, pulling on a pair of light green linen pants and a flowy, pale blue blouse. She scarfed down a croissant before flying into town for work, her heart racing at the idea of being late for headcount. She had slept so deeply after staying up late with Victoria that her body clock had been disturbed.

Rows of perfect houses blurred together underneath her, customized for each angel when they arrived in Heaven.

Packed closely together on the streets in town were endless shops, bakeries, and studios. Many angels chose to spend their endless free time harnessing their gifts, their workspaces a display of their hard work and dedication.

"Good morning, Iris!" Fallon said as she waved to the red-head sitting outside a café before slowing down and lowering herself onto the walkway. It had been a while since Fallon had run into her, and she figured a quick hello wouldn't hold her up too long.

Iris sipped her latte and crossed her legs as she adjusted herself on a white iron bistro chair. "Morning, Fallon! How've you been?" she asked with a kind smile and raised her mug.

"I'm alright," Fallon answered, out of breath. "We should catch up later, I'm running a little behind." She rolled her eyes at herself. "Overslept."

Iris raised her brow. "Up late with Victoria?"

Fallon rubbed the outside of her arm, embarrassed by the truth. "How'd you guess?"

Iris waved her off. "Well, you two *are* together all the time. It's not hard to assume..." She didn't finish the thought.

"Assume what?" She shook her head, waiting for an answer. Fallon's blood turned cold, her hands clammy.

"Nothing! Just that you two are so...close." Her tone seemed honest enough. Harmless.

"Right. Well, I'll see you around." Fallon soared through the sky to the cloud fields.

Upon her arrival, the lead angel, Theo, looked down at his clipboard. His deep-set hazel eyes flicked back and forth between the columns of names until he scribbled over hers with a purple pen and looked her up and down. The honey blonde curls on his head jostled with the movement.

"Busy night?" he teased.

Fallon cleared her throat. "I'm sorry I'm late."

He lifted his broad shoulder in a half shrug, causing the tip of his wing to stir. "I'm not too worried about it. Go ahead and put your things in your locker, and then get out there. Everyone else is already finished with their first two clouds, so really," he bumped her with his elbow, "you gave them a little time to catch up with you."

With a dip of her head and a soft smile, she whispered, "Thank you." Fallon slinked to her locker and shoved her things inside before tying the strings of her white apron around her waist and grabbing the last bucket on the table. She took a moment to collect herself and shake off the unease she felt covering her like a sheet of snow.

She was in Heaven. Everything was perfect.

With that thought in her head, she put on a smile and got to work. As she flew over to an empty patch of cloud, Victoria spotted her from below.

"There you are!" It wasn't long before she dropped what she was doing and flew to catch up with her other half. "Where were you this morning?" I waited outside for you like normal, but when you didn't show, I thought maybe you had to be here early for some reason."

Fallon felt eyes on them already. Harmless, probably. "No, I'm okay. I just didn't wake up when I normally do." She started painting immediately with the hope that her tardiness wouldn't be noticed by every prying angel at the farm.

Victoria stuttered in the air for a breath. "Oh, okay. Well, do you want me to help you get caught up? Teamwork makes the dreams happen, or whatever they say." Her smile was full, but unsure.

"I'm alright, Vic. Thank you, though." Anxious and reeling, Fallon put her head down and continued mindlessly casting brushstrokes while Victoria lingered above. Fallon felt her presence but refused to look. Just when she thought she was alone, Victoria cleared her throat.

"Love you, Lon," she purred, laced with sass.

Fallon glanced at her sheepishly. "Love you too, Vic," she answered low, and went back to painting the same pink area she had already saturated. Victoria hummed to herself, unsatisfied, and flew back to her row of clouds.

After a few deep breaths, Fallon felt enough like herself again to pour her energy into the colors she mixed. She was great at her job, flawlessly blending the most beautiful, vibrant sunsets.

Three clouds later, Theo entered her workspace. "Hey, um..." His hand rubbed the back of his neck. "Whenever you're finished with that one, they want to see you in the archangel building."

Fallon's heart dropped. "Okay, no problem." When his feet lifted barely off the ground, she panicked. "Do you know why?"

"No idea," he said as he turned to look at her. His face said otherwise, and his jaw ticked.

In front of her locker, Fallon tried to school her expression. She was calm, reasonable. She was hardly late. It would be quick and painless, and she'd go home after a successful day.

"Whatcha doin', Lon?"

Fallon flinched so hard, she bit her tongue. "Goodness, you scared me."

"Everything okay? Are you leaving early?" Victoria's eyes tracked all of Fallon's paint supplies in her locker, and her apron on the hook.

She shook her head. "I'm alright. Theo said someone inside wanted to talk to me. I'm not sure why," she confessed with a shrug.

Victoria looked at her, excited. "You're the best painter they have, Lon. They probably want to tell you how proud they are of your dedication!" she squealed as she pulled Fallon in for a hug.

Fallon hugged her back half-heartedly and offered a straight-mouth smile. "Yeah, maybe. I'll see you later?"

"If I'm gone when you're finished, just come over! I'll make us dinner," she told her before giving her a quick kiss on the temple and running off. "Love ya!"

Fallon rolled her shoulders back and braced herself for what she *hoped* was a glowing performance review. "Love you, too," she mumbled to herself.

The massive marble door pushed open at a glacial pace, the chill in her bones steeling the hinges. Inch after inch, she debated pulling back. What had she done wrong? Was one late morning truly enough to earn a talking to?

Soothing, generic music played in the hall. A single, ornate, white rug ran down the center with tall vases of ever-living flowers placed uniformly on either side. At the end of the hall was the lobby, cold yet tasteful. Cream tufted chairs with gold trim sat back-to-back in short rows. All were empty.

Clicking keys lured Fallon to a white desk floating on its own smaller cloud about 4 feet in the air. A head with lavender hair and horn-rimmed black glasses peeked above a screen.

"Name?"

Fallon cleared her throat. "Uh, Fallon."

A pause, and then more clicking.

"Take a seat, hon."

Fallon's face was unsure. She had never been reprimanded before. "Okay."

Her shoes on marble were deafening in her ears, the keyboard a ticking time bomb. Her butt touched the seat for half a second before a male angel that she didn't know poked his head out of a door she hadn't seen.

"He'll see you now."

Who was she meeting?

She tried to slow her steps, refusing to give this man, who didn't know her, the idea that she felt nervous, or worse, guilty.

She didn't. She had no reason to.

The angel led her down another hallway for seconds that felt like hours. White wooden osoors with no windows or name cards passed in her peripheral vision.

Right as she was about to ask who her meeting was with, the angel turned and twisted a gold doorknob. He waved his arm toward a small violet chair with buttons down the fabric opposite a large brown desk with papers stacked across it. "He'll be in shortly."

After she stepped inside, Fallon's brows pulled together as she raised a finger in question. "Who is—"

The door slammed shut on her question.

Why is it that those requested have to be on time, but the ones they're meeting are on their own schedule?

Fallon tried to stop picking at her nails. She stared at the wilting flower tied around her finger, the one she refused to take off after Victoria gave it to her.

What would Victoria tell her to do?

Take deep breaths, check. List what she can see, check. She couldn't smell anything but the ghost of Victoria's lip balm on her temple.

Vanilla.

She willed that scent to linger in her nose as her body vibrated anxiously.

Far too much time passed before a soft knock sounded at the door. Fallon jumped to her feet when it opened to reveal a male seraph with tired brown eyes and short auburn hair.

"Please, sit."

She did.

"Have I done something wrong?" Fallon had waited for so long that her manners left her. She needed to know why she was pulled aside, why she felt like she could crawl out of her skin.

"Do you *feel* that you've done something wrong, Fallon?"

"I...I don't think so." She bit her lip. "I showed up late for work this morning, but I worked extra hard to make up for it because I felt so bad."

The seraph smiled, warm and calming. "You're not here because you were late for a shift at work."

"Then....why am I here?"

He cleared his throat and lifted a pair of glasses to the bridge of his nose. The click of his pen echoed in the silent white room, and scribbling sounds followed as he wrote on his clipboard. "You are here, Fallon, because we have some questions about your relationship with a Miss—," he flipped through his papers as Fallon's heart sank lower and lower. "—Victoria."

She tried her best to look unfazed. "What *about* my friendship with Victoria?"

He didn't miss how she changed his wording, and looked at her from above the golden rim of his glasses. "The nature of it. Your history together, that sort of thing." His voice was honeyed, like he had no stake in why she was brought in.

"I'm afraid I don't know what you mean." Her heart raced so quickly it could burst through her pale skin.

"That's alright. I'll be handling your case; my name is Dimitri. I've been tasked with observing you, and I have to say, it doesn't bode well for you, Miss Fallon."

Tears threatened to well in her eyes. Her nose burned, the tension in her forehead excruciating. "So, what? You're going to watch me?"

"I already have." He flipped back to the front of his clipboard. "I brought you in here today to get it from, well, the horse's mouth."

"What am I supposed to say? We're friends, we have been for years." Her fingers were practically raw from picking at them.

"And that's all you're willing to tell me?" His forehead creases deepened, trying to pry more information from her.

"There is nothing else to tell."

His pen clicked closed. "Alright." He stood, shoulders wide, his face cool and calm. "If you're not going to be honest with me, there isn't much I can do here. This back and forth isn't going to do us any good."

Fallon's nostrils flared. "Is that it, then? Can I go home?"

As he opened the door to go back into the hall, he glanced at Fallon. "For now."

4

F ALLON KEPT HER CHIN down as she flew home, her eyes shifting around aimlessly, anxiously. She felt the weight of stares on her back, and yet, when she dared to look, she found no one. Dimitri's voice echoed in her head, his questions and their casualness sitting like a thick fog in her mind.

The front door of her home slammed behind her as she gripped at her chest, desperately clawing for something she couldn't find. Her nails left streaks of red on her pale skin, hard enough to leave a mark without breaking skin. She schooled her breath as her hands dropped to her sides. Hold for three, exhale for four. She did that over and over until the numbers began to scramble.

And then, she screamed. Filled with rage, her face turned pink as tears fell down her cheeks, racing each other to the ground. She knew the veins in her forehead and her neck were bulging, her throat already sore. As she continued to cry, she raked through memories of her and her dear friend in scared silence. What could they have seen? Had she not been careful?

A delicate knock sounded at her door, drawing a quick breath from her that her lungs couldn't fill. She quickly wiped away the tears and tried to right herself. Victoria always knew when something was wrong.

After a centering, too-long breath, she opened the door. "Heey," she croaked.

Victoria's eyes were squinted, her mouth open. "What happened to coming by my place? I've been waiting over there for you, is every—,"

Fallon's lip started trembling, and Victoria stopped.

"Fal?" She reached out to rub Fallon's arm, who flinched away.

"I'm scared, dove." She began to sob.

"Whoa, whoa, hey, what happened?" Victoria pushed through the door and guided them to the couch, trying to soothe the tremors wracking her dearest companion. "Is this about the meeting? What did they say?"

"I'm in trouble, Vic," she managed through her sobs. She could barely see through the collection of tears.

"*You're* in trouble? How? What did they accuse you of?" Victoria's face was stern, ready to tell off the person who made this mistake.

"That's the thing, I-I don't know if I've actually been accused of anything. It felt more like a threat."

"Someone *threatened* you? Fallon, who did you meet with? We have to tell the seraphim, this is ridiculous." She started to storm away, likely to pace while she thought of their next steps, but Fallon grabbed her arm.

"You can't get involved." Her voice was solid, no quiver in sight. That was the one thing she knew for sure: she had to keep Victoria out of it.

Victoria scoffed, her brows furrowing. "What do you mean, Lon? I have to help clear your name. Whatever they think you did, we can talk to them! We can—"

"I think they might be right." Fallon refused to meet her eyes.

Victoria's worry lines grew evident, her chest rising and falling at a quickened pace. "I don't understand." She shook her head. "What did you do? I can help you fix it, Lon," she pleaded as she again reached out to caress Fallon.

Fallon flinched, but didn't move away this time. She forced her eyes up to meet Victoria's gloomy ones and bit her lip before saying something she never imagined. "I can't tell you."

It was as if Victoria had been struck. "We tell each other everything. What do you mean you can't tell me?" Her mouth fell open as she fumbled to find the words. "Fallon, I can help you! This isn't the time to shut me out. If someone is threatening you, we need to talk to—"

"You can't help me! Stop trying to *fix* everything, alright?" Fallon took a step back and turned away. "Just go..." She didn't mean to say it. The words tore through her like she had taken a bread knife from the kitchen and plunged it into her chest. The sound that came from her broke Fallon's heart even further than her own words. She felt Victoria behind her, felt her reach out, and then felt her turn toward the door.

Alone again, Fallon fell to her knees in the center of her living room, the thud echoing in the silence of her home. Her hands covered her face as she wept until the light coming through the windows faded to black.

When she woke the next morning, the effort it took to open her eyes was nearly enough to put her to sleep again.

Dried tears sealed her lashes together, her lids so swollen that her vision was obstructed. Fallon trudged to the kitchen and secured an ice pack, usually intended for her picnic basket, to help the puffiness in her face. If she was supposed to go on like normal and avoid any further suspicion, she couldn't look bothered. She needed to blend in. Be *normal*.

Fallon had never been normal a day in her life.

She had always been in Heaven, had grown up in the beauty of the clouds, and been surrounded by serenity. She had everything to be grateful for, which meant she had everything to lose. The accusation against her was world-shattering, and she couldn't afford to start over. After centuries of peace and love and perfection, she was losing it. Her mind, her relationships, any remaining hope.

So she had to try, she decided. Even if she had to plaster a smile on her face, and cast a windstorm beneath her wings to keep herself upright, she would manage. She could recover from this. She *had* to recover from this. How hard could it be to completely change her thoughts and feelings?

After mindlessly getting ready for work, she flew at a snail's pace until she reached the cloud fields. She was early; only two other angels had arrived before her. They both looked at her and quickly looked away when their eyes connected.

Fair enough, she thought.

Fallon wasn't surprised that others had heard about her meeting yesterday. While they surely don't know details, everyone has secrets and eons of free time—rumors fueled the world, even in the afterlife. They no doubt all had theories about why Fallon had been called out of work before going home in distress. She stuffed down every negative feeling she had and dug into her dwindling well of passion as she began to paint through her emotions. Agony-fueled reds and anxious oranges carried into every cloud she worked on. Purple made its appearance as the edges of her vision began to blur, the wall of despair threatening to spill tears down her cheeks after hours of holding firm.

"Lookin good over here." Victoria's voice was soft, reaching.

Fallon briefly looked over her shoulder and then back at her work. "Thank you."

A moment later, her dove's chest nearly brushed her arm. Her head dipped toward Fallon's ear. "Can we talk about last night, please? I didn't like leaving that way."

Fallon closed her eyes for a beat as her forehead wrinkled. "Not now, Vic."

"Then when?" Her volume had raised only a hair, but Fallon eyed her anyway. She sighed, but lowered her voice. "You kick me out, and then leave for work before our usual meet-up time. I can't work without knowing you're okay."

Her fingertips grazed Fallon's elbow. "That *we're* okay." She delicately moved a lock of hair behind Fallon's shoulder.

She gritted her teeth to prevent herself from leaning into it. "I need to focus right now. We can talk later."

"Promise?"

Her uncertainty made Fallon's heart ache. "Yes, I promise." She pulled herself away from her buoy and tried to float on her own. She wanted to lose herself in her painting, which was impossible with Victoria standing right next to her.

Fallon spared a glance in her direction.

With crossed arms and a raised brow, she knew how to get to her.

"Promise," Fallon said again.

With a dissatisfied huff, Victoria returned to her workstation.

The heaviness on Fallon's back didn't disappear when her dove did. She went deathly still as she tried to sense where the cause of her unease was coming from. After a moment, her head twisted to look at the balcony of the archangel building she had been called into the day before; it was visible from the cloud farm. Her heart sank as she looked up at the seraph holding her life in his hands—Dimitri. Her lips parted in silent shock before she quickly turned away again.

Was he going to watch her like that every day? Although she supposed, he already had been.

Knowing he saw that interaction with Victoria made her skin crawl. Who was he to intrude on a private conversation between friends? He didn't know anything; nothing was going on between them. She would prove it to him.

If she could prove it to herself first.

Victoria found her after everyone had hung up their aprons and cleaned their brushes, as she always did. "Can we do dinner tonight, please? I had all these plans yesterday, and then it went sour, and if I have to look at everything again tonight and can't use it, it's going to brea—"

"Okay, okay! I get it, I'll come over."

She sighed, relieved. "Good. Thank you." She took Fallon's hands in hers for a brief moment and then walked off. "See you later!" she called out.

Before she could step into Victoria's home again, she had to face Dimitri, tell him to back off, and leave them alone. Victoria was right, after all, he couldn't threaten her.

Set on her plan, Fallon stormed into the marble building that seemed to swallow dreams and snuff out fires. Her shoes clicked on cold tiles as she marched up to the floating desk that held all the answers she needed.

"Where is Dimitri?" No pleasantries, this time. She was on a mission.

That same angel with lavender locks looked over her screen, down to the steaming angel in front of her. "Do you have a meeting?"

"No, but—"

"Take a seat," she clipped, and went back to typing far more than necessary for the level of traffic in the building.

Fallon looked up at the ceiling and groaned, but obeyed. She sat in the same seat she had chosen the day prior and waited for someone to call her. That is, until she decided she was done waiting.

"Where is the restroom?" she called from her chair.

The head of lavender hair extended an arm and pointed toward a brightly lit hall.

"Thanks," Fallon clipped, and started in that direction.

She opened every door looking for Dimitri, unable to remember which office was his, when finally she came upon a door with shuffling noises behind it. She wrapped her knuckles on the white wood lightly.

"Come in," the masculine voice said.

Bingo.

Fallon whipped open the door and sat at the lush, deep violet chair across from his desk. "Must you insist on watching everything I do? Do you truly have nothing better to do with your time?"

Dimitri pulled his pair of thinly-rimmed gold glasses from his nose and placed them on his desk. "That would be my job, Miss Fallon."

"What, to stalk me? To follow me? It's unfair, and unsettling."

He propped an ankle on top of his knee, crossing his leg, his navy pant leg lifting to reveal a pair of shiny, light gray loafers. "Do you have anything to hide?"

"No, but—"

"Then why is it an issue if I follow you? Since you have nothing to hide..." He tilted his head and pursed his lips.

"Because it's invasive. If there's such an issue with the way I behave, then why am I allowed to roam free, hm? If I'm such a *danger* to our society that I need to be stalked, I'd be kept away from it."

Dimitri looked at her for a moment, and he smirked, his brows lifting. "You make a great point, Miss Fallon."

She hadn't expected that answer. Fallon straightened her shoulders and laced her fingers on her lap. "Okay."

"Such a great point, in fact, that I won't be following you anymore."

Relief flooded Fallon like a tidal wave. "Thank you," she said. She stood and smoothed her skirt. "If that's—"

"You'll be staying here under my observation."

5

ONE HOUR TURNED TO two, and then three. Victoria grew antsy as their dinner plans slipped away. She checked her clock again to make sure she wasn't losing her mind.

Fallon really *was* incredibly late.

"This is so unlike her," she mumbled to herself. She tried to fight the urge to bite at the lifted skin around her nails, and she failed. Mid nibble, she talked herself into walking back over to Fallon's house to check again. They had keys to each other's homes, so she could easily let herself inside. Victoria did just that, looking in every room of the house. When her search turned out Fallon-less, her breath came quicker and her heart beat so loud, she thought their neighbors might hear it. Victoria's hand rested on her forehead as she tried to slow her breathing, thinking of logical explanations for her friend's tardiness. She paced in circles, driving herself mad with worry as she made a mental list of all the things that could have prevented Fallon from coming home to her.

"Maybe she got lost—or, or, maybe she fell and can't fly and got picked up by medics, but I'm her emergency contact, so they would've called me by now..." She continued talking herself into a frenzy while her hands got shakier and clammier. "Deep breaths, Victoria. You're a rational person, so think rationally. Where was she last?" she asked the empty house.

In a moment of clarity, Victoria snapped and yelled out, "The cloud farm!" Her palm met her forehead as she scoffed. "Of course, she got caught up at work. I'll find her there." Victoria flew out of the house without grabbing any of her things. She had no time; she needed to find Fallon and ease the aching in her chest that grew in her absence.

Several angels gave her strange looks for moving so quickly in the evening—no one had anywhere to be after sunset. Others tried to wave politely, but she was unable to meet them with her usual cheer. She couldn't stop for small talk, not for anything. When she arrived at the cloud farm, every apron was hung and accounted for. The paintbrushes were in their cups, ready to grace the skies with *unlimited potential,* as the seraphim referred to it.

It was almost eerie, the lack of noise coming from their usually bustling workspace.

"Hello?"

She received no reply, which made the hairs on the back of her neck stand on end. Victoria's brows pinched as she took her bottom lip between her teeth. Her hand moved up and down her arm, trying to flatten the goosebumps that formed.

"Fal?" Her voice rose as a feeling of *wrong* crept over her. She checked every aisle of lockers, but Fallon was nowhere to be seen. Victoria decided she should speak to a seraph... Maybe it was nothing, and she was just getting in her head.

Or, maybe she wasn't.

Victoria pushed through the heavy, gilded doors into a marble room with comfortable-looking chairs. An unfamiliar face sat at a desk atop a cloud several feet above the spotless floor. "Excuse me?"

The angel's face shot up at the intrusion. "Can I help you?" she snapped, surprised by her presence.

"Maybe," Victoria said as politely as she could. She needed help, whether they were nice or not. "I'm looking for my friend. She has blonde hair, blue eyes, fair skin, about my height. Have you seen her?"

She looked back down. "I see a lot of people."

Victoria couldn't help it, she scoffed. "Well, she's *missing*, so if you wouldn't mind actually being helpful, I'd greatly appreciate it."

She slowly raised her head and looked Victoria up and down with a raised brow. "This is Heaven, doll. People don't go missing."

Victoria groaned, her frustration brewing. "But she *is*. Did you see her or not?"

The angel huffed. "Name?"

"Fallon. She also responds to Fal, Lonnie, Lon and, occasionally, Bun."

Victoria hadn't noticed because she was listing Fallon's nicknames, but the angel was eyeing her in a way that made her stomach flip.

"Bun?"

Victoria cleared her throat, her hands moving as she spoke. "Yes, um.. Cinnamon bun—bun. I make her a cake of cinnamon buns every year for her birthday because it's the only thing I—"

"I don't need all the details of your life, doll," she interjected as she looked through her papers. She squinted for a moment, and then a cold expression took over. "Let me ask around. Go take a seat."

Victoria looked over the room and settled on a chair two rows over from the desk. She crossed her legs and bounced her foot anxiously while she absorbed her surroundings. It wasn't a friendly room; it looked like it meant business. Victoria sniffled and tore at the broken skin on her lip as she fiddled in her seat, desperate for answers. Not two minutes later, a door slammed and footsteps pounded on the marble until she saw a face. A stoic-looking male seraph with a sharp-angled face and blonde hair walked directly toward her with purpose.

When he was three feet away, a sweet smile appeared on his face as he extended his hand. "Victoria, I presume?"

"That's me." She met his hand with a gentle greeting and explained her situation. "—hours went by, and I hadn't heard from her. I looked around her house and didn't find her there; this is very unlike her, and I'm worried."

His lips pursed as he contemplated. "You checked her home?"

She nodded. "I did. I have a key, so I went and poked around but didn't find anything."

"An extra key," he repeated as his eyes widened. "How convenient."

"Right..." Victoria didn't like the look in his eyes or the way his smile didn't reach them, but she needed his help. "So, do you know where she might be?"

He straightened his spine and pushed out his chest, which made his wings look taller. "As a matter of fact, I do. If you could come with me, please," he requested as he stood, and motioned for her to follow him.

"Oh, thank goodness!" Victoria put a hand to her chest and felt hopeful. Fallon was alright after all, she had simply overreacted. "I was really starting to worry. Where is she?"

He placed a hand on Victoria's shoulder. "I'll take you to her, don't worry."

Victoria smiled at him gratefully and followed him through a maze of hallways, down several flights of stairs. "This building is massive. You'd have no idea from the outside!"

"Yes, well, there is often more going on that we cannot see."

Just as Victoria was about to ask how much longer their journey would be, he stopped in front of a door and pulled out a ring of keys. He found the right one immediately, despite the number of options, and ushered her inside, where there was—

Nothing. Nothing but a single wooden table and two white chairs in a windowless room, void of color.

"I'm confused. I thought you said Fallon was here." She turned to look at him, her face twisted.

The seraph remained in the doorway. "She is," he nodded. "Not in this room, but a different one."

She chuckled and crossed her arms. "Okay, well, can I see her?"

He clasped his hands in front of him. "Not yet, I'm afraid. You see, Fallon is being questioned."

"Questioned?" Her pitch rose. "If this is about her work ethic or performance, I can *assure* you she is the best painter in Heaven. Someone is lying, she would never do—"

"I'm sure you're *very* familiar with her, Miss Victoria." He took a step back and selected another key from the ring. "You'll need to wait here until she's been cleared to speak with you. If I were you...I'd get comfortable." The door slammed before she could ask any further questions.

Victoria stared at the closed door, mouth agape. After collecting her thoughts, scrambled as they were, she took one single deep breath to calm herself, which failed. She resorted to thinking out loud, whether or not anyone could hear her. "This is ridiculous, you know. You can't keep us locked away, we didn't do anything wrong!"

She was met with silence.

"Heelllloo," she yelled into the empty room, her tired, confused voice echoing back at her. "I'm going to report you!" she threatened. To whom or what, she didn't know.

Victoria screamed and called out for anyone to tell her what was going on, to let her out. No one replied.

In another room, two floors below, Fallon sat in complete silence. They'd given her no chair in her small confinement, but graced her with a hard cot in the corner. She opted to sit on the floor with her legs pulled to her chest. Layers of her long blonde hair fell over her shoulder, some of them blocking her vision. She didn't move them.

She hadn't uttered a word since they locked her in the cell. Nothing she said would change their minds about her anyway—nothing short of a lie.

Hours drifted by without a sound in the cold, white marble room. The lights were too bright for her to sleep, and she knew the moment she drifted away, they would wake her. It wasn't worth it. Instead, Fallon thought. It was all she felt capable of doing, spiraling about her uncertain future.

Her last interactions with Victoria drifted through her mind while she traced the faint currents flowing through the marble. She had been mean. Short. Unforgivable. Had Victoria noticed that she wasn't herself?

Of course she did. She *had* to, Fallon thought. No one knew her like Vic. She had never doubted that before, and she didn't plan to start.

Her nails were ripped down to the skin; she had torn at them so much. The skin around her nailbed had become puffy and red from her picking at them. Her flower ring was gone; they took it from her when they locked her away. Fallon knew she relied too much on Victoria, not as a crutch, but as a safe place. Victoria never made her feel strange or rushed or dim, she made her feel grounded. She had made peace with it, finding comfort in knowing that someone always had her back. Someone she trusted with everything in her heart; someone she trusted *with* her heart.

Someone she loved.

6

FALLON WAS WRONG.

They didn't wake her when she slept; they *watched* her. She opened her eyes and immediately startled, jolting and smacking her head against the wall by her cot.

Dimitri was in her cell. He didn't move or look away when she woke; he simply stared at her.

"Sleep well?" he asked, as chipper as ever.

Fallon groaned and rubbed her hand down her face. "You know I didn't."

Dimitri shrugged with a tight smile. "You never know, you know. They say guilty men can't sleep," he wagged a finger at her.

"I am not guilty," Fallon managed to mumble.

"Sorry, what was that?"

"I am not GUILTY!" she snapped, as she slammed her hand against the wall.

"Hm. Lashing out," Dimitri said as he scribbled onto a pad of paper.

"Why are you in here?" Her voice trembled, no louder than a whisper.

"Isn't that obvious? I'm here to watch over you, to make sure you aren't further staining yourself."

Her face twisted. "Nothing about me is *stained.*" She wrapped her arms around herself. "You're being hurtful."

Dimitri pointed his finger at her, accusingly. "What's hurtful is you lying to me, lying to your friends, and, more importantly, lying to yourself. Just come clean, Fallon. We can help you, and you can leave this place."

Her eyes shifted, cautious. "I can leave?"

He nodded, too eager. "Yes, yes, of course. I just need you to tell me the truth, and you can go on your way."

Fallon looked down at what remained of her nails and thought of how worried Victoria likely was. "I want to speak to Victoria."

The dry chuckle that came from him didn't give her any confidence. "I thought you might."

A loud click sounded from the door of her cell before it creaked open, and she got a glimpse of familiar golden-hued skin.

Fallon shot up from her cot, desperate. "Victoria?" Tears welled in her eyes as her beloved friend fully turned the corner, glossed in confusion.

When her eyes landed on Fallon, they grew wide, and she practically ran the short distance to her. "Fallon! My goodness, I was so worried."

The two became tangled in one another as Fallon turned her head into Victoria's neck, and her hand went into the dark hair she so deeply missed.

"I know, Vic. I'm so sorry about how I left things with you. I was rash and rude, and it was uncalled for. You could never do anything to make me angry. You know that, don't you?"

Victoria pulled away just enough to put eyes on Fallon. "What are you going on about? I haven't seen you for two days, and you start apologizing to *me?* Why are we even here? I've tried to explain to them that we didn't do anything wrong and that—"

"Wait," Fallon dropped her hands to Victoria's arms and peeked over at Dimitri, who hadn't left the room like she'd hoped. "What do you mean, '*we*'? They kept you here?"

"Fallon, seriously, what's going on?" She shook her head in disbelief, sure that it was all a big misunderstanding.

She stormed over to Dimitri and clenched her jaw to retain her composure. "You told me this was about *me*. She has nothing to do with this; she shouldn't be here." She knew her face had reddened, she could feel it. Before he said anything, she whipped back to Victoria. "You need to get out of here."

"Fallon, *please*, you're scaring me." Her nostrils flared as she reached for Fallon's hand. "Let's just deal with this and go home, alright?"

"She can go when she decides to be honest with me," Dimitri said from the middle of the doorway. "Time is ticking, Fallon. Have you decided?"

Fallon's eyes lingered as she looked over Victoria, checking for signs of distress. Cuts, bruising, anything. After she was satisfied that her dove hadn't been harmed physically, she deigned to look at him. "She goes home, and we talk."

His smile didn't shift. "Done." He snapped, and two large angels shoved their way into the room. Their wings stretched so wide that they had to enter the door sideways. Before Fallon could blink, each of them grabbed one of Victoria's arms and started to pull her back out of the room.

"Fallon?! What did you agree to?" Victoria's face scrunched with concern as she tried to wrestle her arms free.

"Please don't worry, dove, it'll be okay. I'll come home soon, I promise."

The door slammed behind Victoria, and the look Dimitri gave Fallon made her stomach twist. "You shouldn't make promises you can't keep."

"You said that if I came clean, I could go home." Her fists clenched at her side as she ground her teeth.

Dimitri tsked and quirked his lip. "*No*, Fallon, I said that you can leave. Someone with your...affliction can't stay here. It stains the community," he explained. "You understand, of course." He stalked forward and clamped a hand on Fallon's shoulder. "And then to repeatedly lie about it all?" He circled her. "Heaven is not the place for someone with these burdens."

Fallon's heart sank lower and lower the longer he spoke. "You aren't serious. I'm as low as murderers and rapists? Philosophers and tyrants?" Her voice grew louder as her anger bubbled not so far below the surface.

He looked at her with a strange kindness in his eyes—like he thought he was helping her.

She was incapable of piecing together a plea, so she stared, unblinking.

"Wipe that look off your face, please. I can't lead you through the halls looking so...disturbed."

Fallon didn't mean to scoff. "I'm sorry I don't look well enough for you to banish me from my rightful place in—"

He struck her, hard and unforgiving. Her mouth fell open as her cheek reddened and stung. "You bite your tongue." He adjusted the collar of his shirt. "You have no right to say such things. You were *allowed* to be here. Don't make this worse for yourself, alright? For poor Victoria..." he trailed off.

At the mention of her dove, Fallon's jaw and fists clenched in tandem. "Don't say her name. You don't deserve it."

"And you've proven you don't deserve the wings gracing your flesh, but that will be remedied shortly. I'm warning you," he told her as he pointed his finger in her face.

Tears threatened to spill from her eyes. It took every ounce of strength she still had not to scream for Victoria to come back, to beg for help, and apologize again. But she knew what that would do to her dove, and she couldn't take that risk. Instead, she straightened her shoulders and raised her chin. She would not be made a villain.

When Dimitri realized what she had decided, he grabbed her bicep and led her out of the room. She didn't fight, she didn't budge, not even as strangers slowly exited the rooms lining the halls. She made eye contact with none of them. Her heart slowed the further they walked from her cell toward her impending demise.

She knew where they were headed when she saw the door. It was taller than the others and had thick bars caging a small window in the center. It was a gloomy gray color, different than the crisp white of every other door in the building. Fallon took a deep breath in an attempt to calm her nerves. There was no changing her mind.

She was sure her only options were this or death.

In death, she would never see her dove again. She was unsure if damnation had the possibility of them meeting again, but Fallon told herself that even a small chance was better than nothing.

With a final step, she arrived at her final decision. Dimitri opened the door with one of his many keys and let her walk through the doorway herself. The walls inside were the same color as the door, drab and cruel. Rows of white benches surrounded a stone block three feet wide and two feet tall. Remnants of red stained the top and scattered the floor around it. The weight on her back became unbearable. Without thinking, she wrapped her arms around herself and grazed over the base of her wings. Goosebumps covered her arms and shoulders as she pictured her new reality. She began to grieve the life she was about to lose, the friendships she valued, and the community she had built in a place that she so dearly loved.

And yet, in that moment, Fallon knew in her heart that she had made the right decision. She was not afraid of what might come next. The only thought in her head as she knelt with her back to the stone was Victoria's face. Her pink cheeks, her rich brown eyes, the way her nose turned up at the tip, and the way it turned red when she got cold. She pictured the flyaways that always left her braid and the way her framing pieces separated when she was warm or sweating. Fallon closed her eyes and sifted through her memories until she found the most comforting one.

It was raining. It wasn't unusual for heaven to be pecked with wet kisses, but that day felt different. She and Victoria had met for lunch at a park. They were the only two at the park that day; for some reason, the others didn't like to get their wings wet. Victoria loved it; she said she felt alive spinning in the rain. She imagined she was being washed clean by the Heavens, and it made her feel rejuvenated.

The two of them took turns hiding, while the other sought them out. No place was off limits; the two climbed trees and crawled through culverts, trying to delay being found. Fallon always found her, though. Victoria loved the game even though she wasn't good at it. On that particular day, Fallon took her time looking. She wanted Victoria to think that she had bested her. She knew the exact tree that she hid behind, and yet she waited. When it started to rain harder, she crept around the massive trunk and slammed her hand next to Victoria's head.

"Got you!"

Victoria's eyes grew wide as she yelped, and her hand gripped her speeding heart. "Good gracious, you scared me!" she yelled with a chuckle.

Fallon couldn't help but laugh. With no one watching her, she threw her head back and cackled. "I don't know why you're surprised. I'll always find you, Vic."

Those brown eyes squinted at her claim. "Always is a strong word."

Fallon crossed her arms. "I meant it," she teased. "You can't hide from me."

Victoria reached forward and uncrossed Fallon's arms before putting them around her, connecting them. "I believe you," she muttered against Fallon's cheek. "I believe you."

With that afternoon replaying in her head, a small smile grew on her face. It disappeared when Dimitri's voice boomed, echoing in the dim room. She hadn't noticed them come in, but the angels that lined the hall now sat on the benches, circling her.

"Fallon. You are charged with having impure thoughts about another female angel. You have tainted the sanctity of those around you by doing so and will be sentenced to banishment. Do you have anything to say for yourself?"

Fallon took that moment to take in the angels who looked down upon her. She traced their faces and committed them to memory as she stirred on her next words.

"I confess to having romantic thoughts about another angel. I do not agree with the idea that this makes me less deserving of my place here. I hope that you feel at peace with your actions, as I feel at peace with mine." A tear ran down her cheek, but her voice did not falter. "I don't agree that this is fair, or right, but...I accept my fate for what it is. And I am not sorry."

She looked to the ceiling and lifted her chin. Another tear dropped to the floor as she reached around to collect her hair and pull it over her shoulder. Before she could do anything else, she felt Dimitri grip her right wing near the skin of her back, and she tensed.

And then he wrenched it from her body.

It felt like hot iron being shoved into her shoulder blade.

The scream that erupted from her throat was bloodcurdling and hoarse. She didn't feel the blood run down her back, but rather, saw it drip onto the floor around her knees. Fallon couldn't move as she stared down at the crimson that marred her skin. When she tried to catch her breath, she felt him tug on her left wing. A sob broke free as he changed his hand position and yanked again, fully ripping the wing from her flesh.

The last thing she saw before falling to the floor was the blood pooling beneath her body. Then, she saw nothing.

7

NO ONE WOULD ANSWER her questions. They wouldn't even look her in the eye, which made her stomach sink.

Victoria ran from angel to angel, pleading with them to tell her what was going on.

"What did she agree to?" she cried. "Why can't I see her?"

They all turned away, or pretended they didn't hear her at all.

After it became crystal clear she would get no more answers, she wiped the stray tear that had snuck its way down her cheek, and flew faster than she ever had back to her home. When she arrived, she slammed the door behind her and leaned against it, sliding slowly until she reached the floor. There, she broke completely. She knew in her gut that something had happened to Fallon. She could *feel it.* And in the silence of her home, she wept. Without Fallon to soothe her shaky breaths, she cried until her eyes were puffy and her throat was raw.

She finally composed herself enough to stand and went to her kitchen sink. The small window above it looked right at Fallon's house, where there was no sign she had ever come home after that day at work.

Despite her worst efforts, Victoria spent the rest of her evening consoling herself and picking weeds in her garden. The sunset came and went, and she still knelt by her garden bed with sweat on her brow and dirt packed under her nails. In the fresh dark of dusk, she pulled her hands from the soil and looked at them. They painted each other's nails often, and her polish had started to chip; with no Fallon to fix them.

Awoken from her gardening frenzy, Victoria ran to her bathroom and turned it upside down trying to find her nail clippers. Rolls of tissue and various products were scattered on the floor, filling the space until she found them in the last drawer in the cabinet. She quickly cut down all of her nails, which had, at one point, been beautifully manicured by her other half, until the silver clippers reached the skin of her finger. When she looked at her nails in the light of the moon, she couldn't see the chipped paint anymore. The parts of her nails with polish peppered her vanity and sink, and only then did she take a deep breath. As she inhaled, she shook. As she exhaled, she cried.

She barely slept an hour the whole night. Every time she closed her eyes, she saw the pain on Fallon's face as the guards pulled her away.

At first light, Victoria pulled her hair into a ponytail and soared through town. She needed answers, and she was going to get them.

She arrived at the large marble doors with red cheeks, puffy eyes, and half of her hair fallen out of its style. She didn't bother fixing herself before hauling the door open and marching up to the floating desk.

"Where is she?" she demanded.

The colorful-haired angel with horn-rimmed glasses jumped as Victoria slammed her hand against the front of the desk.

"I'm afraid I don't—"

Victoria was not there to play games with the angel. Her eyes flicked to the right briefly, and she noticed.

"Don't you dare—"

Victoria had already taken off toward where the guards brought her yesterday. She opened several incorrect doors, startling the angels working in their offices, before she arrived at the final one.

"Ah! There you are. I was wondering how long it would take for you to come back," Dimitri admitted.

"What did you do with her?" Victoria demanded.

He looked at her with worry in his eyes. "Everything that has happened, Fallon did to herself."

Victoria walked further into the room until her hips were flush with the desk. "I don't believe you. I want to see her. Why is she still here?"

"She isn't here, Victoria. She left this place last night." He was calm, as if the day were like any other.

"That's impossible. She didn't come home last night. I looked for her, I would've known if she went back to her house."

Dimitri stood from his chair, his wings fanning out to his side in a stretch. "Why don't we talk somewhere else. I have a few questions to ask you, Miss Victoria."

"I'm not going anywhere with you," she said before crossing her arms.

"Suit yourself. I thought you might want to know more about what happened with your dear friend," he offered as he left the room, leaving the door open behind him.

Victoria's breath hitched before she followed him out the door and into the hall. After several turns, she found herself in the same room she had been thrown into before when she sought out Fallon. This time, there was a pad of paper on the table in the middle of the room, and the same two chairs.

"What is this?" Dimitri took a seat, and Victoria followed suit. "I thought you said I would learn more about what happened with Fallon."

"You will," he assured her with a click of a pen. "What was your relationship like?"

Victoria squinted. "She's my best friend," she said with a shrug. "We practically live together even though we have separate homes."

He scribbled on his pad without looking at her. "You slept at each other's homes?"

"Sleepovers are kind of our thing. We'll make dinner and then watch a movie until one of us falls asleep. Usually it's me... It's nice." A smile crept onto her face for the first time since seeing Fallon yesterday. "What does this all have to do with what happened to her?"

The scribbling stopped. "It's all relevant, I assure you."

She let out a heavy sigh.

"How long did you two know each other?"

Victoria bit her lip, trying to remember. "It feels like eons."

He peeked up at her. "I need a number, Victoria."

She cleared her throat and fidgeted with the hem of her dress. "One, two centuries, maybe?"

"Maybe?"

"Time moves differently with her," she shrugged. "When you've been in heaven for as long as we have, your perspective of days passed shifts. So, *yes*, maybe."

Dimitri scribbled something else down, his moving pen the only sound in the room.

"And what about your romantic relationship?"

Victoria's head cocked, her heart stalling. "Our what?"

"Please don't make me repeat it, Miss Victoria. It's been a very long couple of days."

"We're friends," she clipped.

"Yes, I'm well aware of that. But when did your friendship evolve into something immoral?" He didn't look up at her.

Victoria insisted, "Our friendship is perfectly moral." When he said nothing, she continued. "I'm having trouble understanding how this is any of your business." She couldn't resist the urge to readjust her crossed legs. She felt her skin crawling beneath the watchful eye of the seraph.

The pad of paper hit the table so suddenly that Victoria jumped. Dimitri took a deep breath with closed eyes before continuing. "It is my job to ensure that Heaven stays unsul-lied and safe. I cannot have angels disrupting the peace we work so diligently to maintain. All that running amok causes chaos."

With a shaky voice, Victoria asked what she needed to know. "Where is Fallon?"

"She left Heaven."

He said it so casually, Victoria thought she had gone in-sane. "That's impossible."

"I'm afraid not. When an angel sullies this place with im-pure thoughts to the point of committing blasphemy, they lose the most gracious opportunity in the history of, well, anything. She had to be dealt with."

Victoria gawked at him. "Fallon is respected in our com-munity! She's talented and—"

"—And that means nothing in the eyes of the seraphim."

She stared at him with her mouth agape. "You think that Fallon..."

"We don't think, Miss Victoria. She confessed."

Victoria's eyes welled with more tears. He had to be mis-taken. "That's not true," she muttered. "We—we're good friends, nothing more."

"I'm glad you feel that way." He placed his pen on the table next to the pad of paper. "I'm thankful we got to speak today; you've made my job much easier by coming to find me. You can return home." He rose from his chair with a friendly nod and turned to leave the room.

"Where did you send her?" Victoria managed around the lump in her throat.

Dimitri froze before the door and looked over his shoulder. "You cannot go after her."

She fought the tears threatening to fall down her cheeks. "I just...I need to know."

His chest rose and fell before he spoke. "She's on Earth."

Her dinner that night tasted bland. Her couch didn't feel right beneath her. She felt *heavy*, like she would sink beneath the fibers and into the dense clouds that held them above an unforgiving world; a world that would swallow the closest friend she ever had.

What they said...

It couldn't be true; Fallon had to have been falsely accused. But the seraphim didn't make mistakes; they were helpful and trustworthy. She had no reason not to believe them.

Victoria thought back to the sort of argument that had happened before she got taken away.

Fallon said she thought she was guilty. If the seraphim banished her from Heaven for impure thoughts, and Fallon said she was guilty...

There was no way.

Dimitri questioned their relationship. She knew her better than anyone; she would know if their relationship was—well, something else. At least, she thought she would. Now, she wasn't so sure.

Victoria spent the next several days trying to wrap her mind around the idea that Fallon was gone. Her house had been emptied, and Victoria's heart felt tied to it. All character of the house had been stripped away: the stones that led from Fallon's home to her own were now gone, leaving Victoria's stones unfinished. Her stained-glass paintings in the windows had been washed away, along with any sign of her existence. It felt wrong, and it felt fast. Fallon still had an apron at the cloud farm.

Dimitri said that she couldn't look for her on Earth, so that left their chances of seeing each other again incredibly slim. She would try anyway, she thought. To clear her name, to find answers, for confirmation, maybe all of the above.

Maybe just to see her face again.

To hug her.

To tell her she loved her.

They would fix this.

8

Her eyes refused to open. She tried and tried without success before she gave up completely. It was barely light out, but Fallon could feel the dull heat of the Sun peeking over the horizon.

She was slick with sweat. Not from heat yet, but from the pain. When she shifted, her muscles screamed in agony. Despite the soft ground, she felt no comfort; the throbbing at her back kept her away from any chance of relief.

Headstrong and incessant, she kept trying to open her eyes anyway. She managed, eventually, and found herself in a field of green. Nothing but clovers and grass and flowers surrounded her for what looked like miles.

It made her chest tight.

It reminded her of Victoria.

Every small, white flower sent a bolt of lightning through the wounds at her back until she felt as if she were made of concrete. She fused with the field, an immovable object.

Fallon baked in the sun as it rose to its peak, and she remained there while it sank again. In her sleep, she felt the whisper of arms around her. She dreamt of being cocooned in a blanket with her dove while they watched movies they had already seen.

Only, when she woke, she was no longer in the field. She was in a house, and a man sat across from her in a wooden chair.

"*Gudskelov*, there you are," he said as he rocked forward on a wooden chair. "I thought maybe you were dead." He put his hands on his thighs and pushed up from the rocker.

She knew she should move; say something, *anything* to this stranger that had seemingly brought her to his home in the dark of night. But she was exhausted, and he looked kind. She closed her eyes again.

Glass clattered in another room, followed by running water. When she forced an eye open to spy, the man put a short glass of water on a small wooden table beside her head. "You can sleep again after you drink this." His accent tugged at something far in her mind, but she couldn't place it.

Fallon shut her eye again so he wouldn't see her, but she was too late.

"You need to drink water, kid. I don't make the rules."

At that, she attempted to sit up. Her head pounded, and she could hardly move her arms.

When she groaned, he stopped her. "You've got a pretty serious injury. I figured you'd be better off not lying in dirt," he told her, which made her bite the inside of her cheek and nod.

"Thank you," she managed through the coarseness in her throat.

He shook his head. "Don't mention it." He looked her over and exhaled sharply from his nose. "Did someone do this to you?"

Her eyes snapped from the tempting glass of water to meet his brown ones, surrounded by creases. He looked older than her, but she knew that was impossible; maybe in his fourth or fifth decade, and had dark brown hair that had become overrun with grey. His skin was tan and wrinkled all the way down to his fingers, like he spent most of his time outside.

Freckles and moles covered his arms and cheeks. With a clenched jaw, she nodded again.

The man pursed his lips and squinted at her. "Alright. I'll leave you alone for a minute." He raised his hands in surrender and started to back out of the room. Before he was through the doorway, he pointed at the glass of water. "Drink that," he told her again, and went back into the other room.

Despite her confusion, she was intrigued. Her first encounter on Earth, and it was...strange. The glass left a ring on the wooden table when she picked it up to inspect it. She held it to the light, looking for anything abnormal. When she decided being poisoned was the least of her worries, she shrugged and drank the entire thing.

An awful, demented noise came from her abdomen. Fallon clutched at her stomach and pondered over why her body was behaving so strangely. Her mouth was dry, her stomach was making strange sounds—

Oh, God. She *had* been poisoned.

The man came back into the room at that moment, startling her. She shifted her weight on the seat she occupied and pulled the blanket tighter around her. Just then, her stomach made the noise again.

He raised an eyebrow at her. "Hungry?"

She tilted her head, contemplated, and nodded.

"I figured you would be," he confessed, and swapped her empty glass with a plate of food. "I hope you like chicken," he quipped, and stroked the hair on his chin before going back into the kitchen to refill her glass. The moment he left, Fallon hurriedly ate what he had given her, finishing nearly half of it before he returned.

When he came back, he sat in his rocking chair and watched her. "Do you have a name?" he asked when she took her last bite.

She stopped chewing for a moment to look him over. "Fallon," she said around a mouthful of food.

He extended his hand in the space between them. "Emil," he offered with a half-smile.

The corners of Fallon's mouth turned up, not quite returning the smile, but something close.

"What brought you all the way out here?"

She licked the front of her teeth to clear any food from them. "Out where, exactly?"

Emil squinted at her as his tongue flicked over his lips before saying, "Ribe." She stared at him in question. "Oldest town in Denmark?"

Fallon leaned forward, astounded. "I'm in Denmark?"

Before Emil could fully process the woman sitting on his couch, she yawned. "You know what, why don't we come back to this later? You get some more sleep, and then I'll tell you anything you want to know."

She yawned again as she rubbed her eyes and nodded. "Okay."

Victoria hadn't eaten anything in days. She felt weak, and her head wouldn't stop hurting.

Her brush had long since run out of paint, but she stared deep into the cloud, unblinking—unaware.

"Victoria," another angel sang at her from the next row over. "You alright over there?"

She jumped, but gave a straight smile. "Yep! Great, thanks."

How were none of them upset?

Victoria was angry. She was grieving her best friend without any help. It was like no one but her even cared that one of their own was gone. Fallon was their best painter, kind and thoughtful with an ever-flowing cup of creativity. Without her, every sunset would be bland. She was able to manipulate color unlike any other angel. Her vibrant pinks and soft oranges were unmatched. And they wanted Victoria to—what, forget all of it?

She refused.

Every night when she returned home from work, she sorted through every picture they had taken together—and there were *a lot*. Victoria was convinced a seraph would come into her home in the night and take them, so every day, she checked. She would know if one went missing. They would not erase Fallon from her history, no matter how they tried to smooth things over and fly forward.

One of the many issues with her plan was that she had no idea how to find Fallon. Earth was massive; she would be looking for a teeny tiny needle in a very big haystack. She would have to miss work—she would need to find someone to tend her garden if she went away.

All of this depended on *finding* her first. She planned to start there.

Every cloud she painted that day was lackluster and muddy. Her color blends were far from seamless, but she managed to tread through her shift. One after the other, her coworkers hung up their aprons and rinsed their brushes before flying home. She took her time, ensuring she was the last one at the farm. When she shrugged on her thin jacket, she had no plans to go home yet.

It didn't feel like home anymore anyway.

With one last look around the workshop, she dipped back into the marble building where the lilac-haired angel sat at her floating desk. Victoria moved like the wind, closing the massive door so gently that it made no sound. Instead of stomping her way down the hall like the last time, she flew along the edge of the wall slowly to not draw any attention to herself. That was something she had noticed before, the poor-sighted angel hardly looked up unless spoken to.

Her heart beat so loud she was sure someone would hear her. Desperate, she ducked into the first hall she came upon. There were fewer doors than the hall she had been down before, meaning she was in uncharted territory. With one final deep breath and shrug of her shoulders, Victoria looked into every room for something that would help her find Fallon. Filing cabinets, records, an abandoned desk, anything that could house information.

When that hall proved fruitless, she poked her head around the corner to look at her options. The next opening was roughly ten feet further down the wall. If she moved quickly, she could be out of the lifeless building before sunset, and anyone left for the day. She readied her wings for another soundless maneuver and raised herself just off the floor when she turned the corner and bumped into none other than the colorful receptionist. It took strength, but she managed not to yelp in surprise.

"Can I help you, miss?" The angel raised a brow over her bright yellow glasses.

"Oh! Yes, I was just um—," Victoria stumbled looking for any excuse to be in this part of the building. "I was looking for the restroom."

The angel craned her neck to see where Victoria had come from. "Right. Well, you can't be back there. These offices are getting ready to close for the night, so don't get stuck in here. Restroom is that way," she said while pointing to a white door that looked just like every other.

Victoria cleared her throat, embarrassed, but thankful that playing dumb erased any flawed intent from her face. "Got it, thank you!" she smiled as she flew toward the door. Once inside, she looked at herself in the mirror for a long while.

"What are you doing?" she whispered at her reflection. "He specifically said you can't go looking for her." She splashed some cool water on her face to bring her temperature down. "You need to go home, Victoria." With her head leaning back against the wall, she closed her eyes to collect her thoughts. When they opened again, they landed on a small row of windows near the top of the wall.

She bit her lip.

"You can't..."

She thought some more.

When she looked back at the mirror, her eyes were wide with something. Hope? Disbelief, maybe?

Victoria sighed. And then she cracked open one of the windows.

With her new plan in motion, she somehow remembered to flush the toilet that had nothing but clean water in it. She ran her hands under the faucet before wiping them on her legs and rushing out the door.

"Thanks again!" she called out as she pushed open the ornate doors that led onto the busy streets of Heaven. She flew home on autopilot without a single thought in her head.

All she had to do was wait.

9

IT WAS DARK WHEN Fallon woke again.

Emil wasn't in his chair or making noise in the kitchen; she figured he was sleeping. Not making noise was difficult in the house; the wooden floors were old and stained, creaking and giving beneath the weight of her bare feet. The only light to guide her was the warm glow of candles Emil left lit, assumedly for her. She picked up the brass candle holder on his coffee table and used it to guide her wandering.

She wasn't a snooper, she was simply...curious. She was in a stranger's house, after all. It was only fair that she knew who he was. There were dozens of photos in various frames, some metal, some wooden. A few of them had portraits of a lone man, while others seemed to be family photos—animals included. She couldn't help but pick up a dark brown frame on the mantel with two men and a dog pictured. The candle provided enough light to see, but not enough to show detail. When she heard a creak to her left, she knew she'd been found.

"Who is this?" she asked, lifting the photo as she turned.

The corner of Emil's mouth pulled into a dull smile. "That's August. And that," he said, pointing at the dog, "is Jesper."

"I haven't seen any animals since being here," she told him.

"There are plenty of animals here, Fallon. You'll meet them all tomorrow." He pat her on the shoulder as he took the frame from her hand.

"And August?" While the thought of meeting someone new made her nervous, she liked his eyes. Something about them was sweet and familiar.

Emil chuckled softly. "I wish you could, kid. You're a few years too late." The sorrow in his voice answered her next question.

Fallon frowned at the photo and stared at the man's face. "I'm very sorry for your loss," she whispered.

"Thank you." He put the frame back on the mantel. "We were together for almost thirty years. He was very sick toward the end; we knew it was coming." Fallon thought she heard him sniffle. "I still miss him every day."

Her shoulders drooped, and her chest felt tight. "I shouldn't have pried. I didn't mean to upset you."

Emil turned to her, face glowing with candlelight. "You didn't upset me, things happen all the time that we don't understand. I have no clue what rational reason the God I knew would have for making August sick, but it happened. I watched him wither away until he could barely remember who he was, let alone the decades we spent together." He took the candle and walked back to the couch she had been sleeping on.

She had no words, but she followed him. She, too, had qualms with their God's actions.

When they sat, he eyed her cautiously. "You look pale."

Fallon laughed. "I always look pale. Just...thinking."

"Well, don't think *too* hard. You'll hurt yourself."

"Emil?" She looked at his profile while he stared at another photo he had on a bookshelf by his rocking chair.

"Yes, Fallon?" He didn't turn his head, but she felt his attention.

"Can I ask you more about him at some point?" There were so many things she wanted to know.

He smiled and dropped his head. "Sure, you can ask more questions. I don't know if I'll have answers for all of them, but, you can ask them."

Fallon nodded. "That's fair."

After a moment of comfortable silence, something rushed to the front of her mind. "What made you bring me in?"

Emil propped an ankle on his knee and rested a hand on it. "The short answer is: you were in my field."

"And the long answer?" she asked through a low chuckle.

He pursed his lips as he debated answering. "August helped anyone. No matter how much help they needed, he was the first to offer a hand. I was always...less willing. After he passed," he paused, "I couldn't let all the effort he made disappear. With him gone, I decided to be someone he would've been proud of." Fallon saw the mist in his eyes, but didn't interrupt him. "He was the best man. The best *person*. It would've been a shame to let that kind of positivity—" his mouth remained open as he thought through his next words— "die with him."

Fallon couldn't help herself. She reached over and placed her hand on his. "I know he's proud of you. Even if I never met him...I know that." She didn't wipe away the tear that fell. She wanted him to see that his actions and words had affected her, no matter how uncomfortable it was for him to vocalize. "Thank you, Emil. I wasn't in the best place when you found me—,"

"In my field."

The laugh that escaped her was loud. "Yes, in your field. But I'm..." She scanned the ceiling as if she could look past it to her home in the sky. "I'm hopeful."

Emil's face twisted with emotion. "Me too, kid. Me too."

Fallon smiled at his choice of words, confident that she was far older than she was. But physically, he was right. The wounds on her back were the first time she had experienced any physical pain, while she knew Emil had seen his fair share from the small scars covering his forearms. "So," she said to try to bridge the gap from their vulnerable moment to something more casual. "How many animals did you say you have?"

"Oh, gosh." Emil wiped his hand down the hair on his chin. "You name it, I probably have one. Sheep, horses, pigs, chickens—"

"That many?!" She whipped her head to look at him.

"This is a farm, Fallon. What else would you suppose I have?"

"Do you—um..." Her head jerked to the side.

"Kill 'em? No, no, not unless I need to. I take whatever they're willing to give me. Eggs, milk, wool, those sorts of things."

Fallon smiled as she stared at him. "You're a kind man, Emil."

He swatted his hand at the air, dismissing her. "Don't go telling anybody."

10

AFTER NIGHTFALL, VICTORIA TOOK the back roads from her house to the seraphim building. Most of her neighbors and friends were inside by that time, and the few she ran into were too busy with their own lives to take much notice of her. Fallon was the more interesting one after all, more talented, although maybe a bit disturbed. Victoria was always happy to tag along.

With adrenaline fueling her, she didn't think twice about flying up to the window she had left open. The issue, though, was that she didn't consider her wings while hatching her master plan. She poked her head through the pane and reached inside to pull the rest of her body through. When she met resistance, she closed her eyes.

"You've got to be kidding," she muttered under her breath.

With everything but her head back outside, she glanced around to see if there were any latches she could reach while stuck on the other side. Blindly, she felt along the edges of the windowsill until her fingers snagged on a small piece of metal. Victoria pulled on it at awkward angles until she felt it shift. The part of the window she was flush with pushed in, and she fell through it. She barely fit through the opening, scraping the tops of her thighs and knocking both her knees. She knew immediately that they would bruise.

She was so overwhelmed by falling through the window that she didn't notice her foot had dipped into an empty toilet until she stood. Her shoe made a horrid squelching sound that sent chills down her arms, and she threw her hand over her mouth to stifle a gag. "Great start..."

Victoria was stubborn. She wasn't going to let a few kinks in her ribbon untie her whole bow; she was determined to find something helpful.

The hall was dark when she exited the bathroom. The moon was enough to light her way, but she didn't know where to start. There were so many offices in this place that she had never seen, probably countless hallways with secret passages and locked doors.

She really hadn't thought this through.

Her teeth tore the skin from inside her cheek as she took in every possibility before deciding to pick somewhere random. If she thought about it for too long, she would talk herself out of it.

Room after room, she delicately sorted through desk drawers and piles of papers, looking for *anything* related to Fallon. She had gone through three hallways before finding a locked office. She looked around in disbelief at what she was about to do. She tensed her shoulder, shifted all her weight to her back foot, and rammed her body into the door.

She stifled a groan when it didn't budge, and her arm hurt.

She tried again and again, alternating her shoulders. Her coworkers would see the bruises on her body, think she got into trouble, and have no idea that it was her own doing. On her sixth attempt, she put all of the feelings from the past week into a ball of rage in her chest and shoved with every aching muscle. When a tiny click sounded from somewhere in the lock, she almost wept.

The knob turned like the mechanism was full of sand, but it opened. When she stepped inside, she was met with stacks and piles of pages taller than she was. She did her best to make a space where she could restack the pages as she picked them up and began skimming each one for any sign of Fallon. She found nothing, and more nothing. By the time she finished going through four stacks, her eyes had started to cross, and the words jumbled on the page.

"This is ridiculous," she groaned when she threw a paper on the ground. One of the pages she disturbed with the mild wind of her throw caught her attention. There it was, in large, plain handwriting.

Denmark, Earth.

Her breath hitched, and her eyes grew wide before she internally yelled at herself to pick it up. There was nothing on the page about Fallon, but it was the first mention of Earth she had seen. She raked over the page until she had nearly memorized it, when something warm touched the back of her shoulder. She turned to see what it was and was blinded by the first morning rays of sunlight. She couldn't believe she had spent her entire night sorting through papers.

She hadn't kept track of the time and, scarily, she had no idea what time the seraphim showed up for their day. Victoria had to get back to the bathroom window, and *fast*. Seraphim had some kind of sense for when something was wrong, and her breaking in to be a living battering ram had to fit the qualifications. She couldn't find where they sent Fallon from the inside of another cell.

Climbing through the window was a bit tougher than falling through it, but she managed, and did so without adding any more cuts or bruises to her tired limbs.

The usual lively morning bustle had started to pick up by the time she made it home. She needed to shower off the embarrassment and shame that had started to settle on her skin before she could face her coworkers. Victoria didn't *snoop*. She didn't lie, she didn't cheat. That wasn't what it meant to be an angel. But, there she was, pulling herself from the ledge of a panic attack because she did those exact things.

It made her stomach turn.

She knew it was wrong, that she should feel sorry. And yet...she knew she had to do it again. *Earth* was not enough for her to up and leave; she had no idea how to get there or where to begin when searching for Fallon. Victoria still doubted what she had seen and heard. She doubted what the seraphim insisted about her best friend. They would prove the seraphim wrong *together*. She just had to find her first.

11

"It tickles!" Fallon laughed as she turned her chin away from the brown cow in front of her.

"Stop movin'! She'll take a bite out of your hand if you keep her from her food."

Fallon's eyes grew wide before whipping to look at Emil. "Will she really?"

He blinked at her slowly and shook his head with a smirk. "Not hard enough to do anything to you. Daisy here takes her food very seriously, though, so don't play with her too much. She might surprise us both." He chuckled as he stroked Daisy's side. "She's gettin' old, but she's still got her sense of humor."

Fallon scoffed. "Sense of humor? Does she tell jokes to you?"

"She doesn't need to; creatures will tell you how they feel without words—their actions, their behavior. Sometimes she looks at me, and I know exactly what she's thinking." Emil didn't look at her, and she was glad for it. She stewed on that for longer than she would've liked to admit.

One by one, the animals ate out of Fallon's hands.

"You know they've got troughs for a reason, right? A lot of them graze on their own; you don't need to hand-feed them."

Fallon shrugged while she inspected the lamb at her side. With one hand full of grain, she used the other to pet the animal. "I know, but it's kind of fun."

"Alright then," he murmured as he clapped the dirt and animal dander off his hands before wandering into the farm.

Fallon didn't realize it, but he disappeared for well over an hour. When he came back, she was still on her knees in the field, surrounded by various farm animals.

"Did you move at all?" His voice startled her so badly, she threw the bits of food in her hand. "Don't go fattening up my animals, Fallon. They're already spoiled."

She wiped her hands on the pair of jeans Emil had supplied her with. They were a couple of sizes too big, but a shoestring turned belt was good enough for her. "They're not spoiled, they're happy. Look at them," she said as she took the lamb's head into her hands. "How can I say no to this face?"

Emil raised a brow and leaned down toward the lamb with his arms crossed. "I do it all the time."

Fallon laughed through her nose. "What do we do now?" she asked as Emil sat down and leaned back onto his elbows with his eyes closed.

"We lay down." Fallon looked at him, head cocked, and he felt her stare. "They're all fed, you picked every weed that's ever thought about growing in my garden, *and* we reorganized the shelves in the barn. You can relax!"

She didn't move.

He opened his eyes to see her fidgeting. "You do know how to do that, don't you?"

"Of course I know how to relax," she lied.

"Yeah?" Emil jerked his head toward the empty patch of grass next to him before closing his eyes again.

Fallon threw him a side-eyed glance and sat cross-legged on the ground. After three deep breaths, she placed her hands on her knees and tried to calm her thoughts.

"You look like a statue," Emil laughed.

Fallon let out an exasperated sigh. "I'm trying, okay?"

"Where did you say you were from?"

Ice settled in her stomach. "I—um," she cleared her throat. "I didn't."

Emil slowly turned his head toward her. "You're not an alien or somethin', are you?"

She chuckled. "No. I'm not an alien."

Satisfied, he turned away. "Good. I read somewhere that aliens eat a lot, and I don't have enough food for all that." With a grunt, he adjusted his arms and took a deep breath. "I'm taking a nap. Since you can't seem to sit still, why don't you go into town?"

Her forehead creased. "By myself?"

He sounded his approval. "I think you can manage that, don't you? Have a little faith.'"

"I guess so," she said, even though she didn't think she could.

"You can take my bike, it's the blue one leaned up against the house. We need new pruners while you're out, so go by Fern's."

"Fern's..." Fallon made a mental note. "Anything else?" she asked when she stood.

He contemplated, pursing his lips. "Something sweet, like some drømmekage or carrot cake."

"You put carrots in your sweets?"

His eyes opened slowly, not caring to move. "I put carrots in everything."

She squinted at him. "Right."

Before she could convince herself that it would end terribly, she grabbed the bike and walked it toward the road. As soon as she was out of sight, she looked down at the contraption. "How on Earth..." Fallon needed to figure out the beast quickly so she wouldn't waste time. She squatted down and poked the tires, then the chain, and the pedals. When the pedal spun, the chain moved, inching the thing forward. The gears began to turn in her head, and she sat on the bike seat. She put her foot on a pedal and gave it a single, mighty push before picking up her legs, sticking them straight out. When she only moved a few feet, she grew frustrated. She didn't allow herself to groan too loudly, regardless of how stupid she felt. She stood from the seat and squatted next to it again, this time pushing the pedal more than once. It looped all the way around, and the more it moved, the further the wheels rolled. Confident she knew what to do, Fallon sat on the seat again and placed her feet on the pedals. With a deep breath, she pushed with one foot, and then the other. She kept pushing until she was flying forward with the wind hitting her face and her hair blowing behind her.

Emil's house shrank in the distance. Fallon didn't know where she was going, but she didn't care. She felt *free*. She never thought she would feel the wind that way again after losing her wings. An ocean of green was all she could see, with the occasional house appearing out of seemingly nowhere. She didn't dare stop. Finding Emil was lucky; she wasn't sure every human on Earth would be as kind or welcoming.

By the time she came upon other buildings, her hair was wind-blown and knotted. The road beneath her was paved with bricks in an arch pattern, tiny flowers and even tinier clover-looking weeds poked through the cracks. If she stared at it too long, it made her feel dizzy. The structures lining the road were all different colors, the yellow shop with a green door standing out the most. On either side of it were white walls with brown accents, worn wooden shutters, and brightly colored flower boxes. Umbrellas stood scattered on the street; some closed, some open with people beneath them.

Fallon stood in the middle of everything, still straddling the bike. No one told her to move or looked at her oddly; they simply went about their business, engaging in conversation with their peers or offering her a soft smile. She waved at a few of them, her confidence brimming after her ride through the countryside. A small, metal grate in front of a yellow wall had two other bikes attached to it. She followed suit and stored the blue bicycle there, when the basket on the back reminded her why she came in the first place. *Pruners and cake* echoed in her head as she stepped through an open green door into a bright, warm space lined with tools and plants of all sizes.

"Velkommen til Bregne's!" a woman called from behind a wooden counter.

Fallon met her stare and offered a small smile. While angels could understand a multitude of languages, her distance from Heaven clouded her memory; she couldn't respond the way she would have been able to in the clouds.

Woven baskets filled with blooming plants filled the shelves. Smaller orange pots had vegetable starters, purple containers housed pink buds, but it was the two white flowers in a vase on the counter that made Fallon stop in her tracks. Her lips parted as she reached out to the flower with a feather-light touch.

"Det er smukt." The woman ducked her head to meet Fallon's eyes, who smiled and nodded. She squinted at Fallon as if she could see inside her brain. "You're not from here," she said in English.

Fallon chuckled. "Is it that obvious?"

"This town is a chatty bunch. You would've asked me a million questions by now." She turned away and rearranged a table of smaller potted plants so the youngest ones were at the back of the table, and the oldest at the front. "I'm Fern, by the way." She didn't extend a hand, too busy organizing her plants.

"Fallon." She stared at Fern's bright blonde hair as the sun shone through the windows, revealing hints of strawberry. Her clear blue eyes were gentle; she looked a lot like Fallon. "You own this place?" Fallon watched her head nod from behind.

"My father named it after me when I was a girl, and passed it down to me. It's sort of a family business." Dirt streaked her apron as she wiped her hands down the front of it. "Is there something I can help you find?"

"Pruners and cake," she said too quickly.

Fern laughed. "Well, I can help with the first part. What size do you need?" she asked, walking toward the back of the shop.

Fallon hadn't thought to ask. "I'm not sure. Emil said he needed new pruners for the farm," she trailed on without thought.

"Emil sent you down here? What, he didn't want to see me today?" Her hands landed on her hips.

Fallon's eyes grew wide. "I'm sure that's not true. He was preoccupied when I left, so I think he just—"

Fern chuckled at her confusion. "I'm only kidding, Fallon. Emil's a regular here; we tease each other. He's friends with my father," she explained. "He's used the same models for as long as we've known him." She grabbed a pair of pruners with green handles and placed them in Fallon's open hands. "Does he need a new trowel, too? He's too rough with it, clanging into rocks without looking."

Fallon found herself fiddling with the pruners. "He didn't say," she mumbled. "I'm sorry, I don't know."

Fern looked at her, worried. "You don't have anything to be sorry for. Here," she picked up a trowel and walked it toward the counter. "I'll have you take one just in case. He'll use it, don't worry."

"Thank you." Fallon's cheeks were warm; she knew she looked silly. At the counter, she couldn't help but stare at the white flower she didn't recognize.

Fern nodded at the plant. "It's beautiful, isn't it? We don't usually carry things from outside Denmark, but I was traveling in Panama this fall and couldn't resist taking a few with me when I left. *Peristeria elata*," she announced as she waved her hand in the sky.

Fallon looked at her, questioning.

"Our guide called it the Holy Ghost orchid, but it's more commonly known as the dove." Fern opened a brown paper bag and placed the gardening tools inside.

Fallon couldn't catch her breath.

"It's in fear of going extinct, so I promised to introduce some buds to our landscape to help them flourish again." Fallon barely heard her above the blood rushing in her ears. Fern grazed a petal with her fingertip before looking at Fallon. "You like it that much?"

She couldn't help the tears that welled in her eyes. "It's wonderful," was all she could manage without them falling. "I know someone who would love it."

Fern pursed her lips and grabbed one of the dishes with the flower in it before scooching it across the counter. "Consider it a gift."

A gasp left Fallon. "I couldn't take this. You brought them here; they're yours. I can't take it," she said again, before pushing it back carefully with a sinking heart.

"You're not taking it, I'm giving it to you. This one could use some attentive care, it isn't doing so well here. Pyt med det, I've got another." She pressed a button on the register and closed it before it could pop open. "Tell Emil I put the tools on his tab."

Fallon nodded sharply. "Thank you."

Fern tilted her head and gave it a light shake. "Tak."

"Tak," Fallon repeated with a smile.

She took her time riding back to Emil's, content being outside in the sun. Fallon appreciated the way it eased the constant chill in her bones.

When she arrived, Emil was standing outside. "Did you find Fern's alright?"

She parked the bike against the side of the house and nodded before holding out the brown paper bag. "I did." She handed the bag over to Emil. "I like her, she's nice. She even gave me this plant as a gift," she said as she held it up between them.

"Oh yeah? I don't know how to care for those things, so that's your own project." He looked in the basket for something else. "No cake?"

Fallon's hand flew to her mouth. "I'm so sorry! I was so excited about the flower, I forgot to go to the other store..."

He could sense the genuine disappointment in her voice, and it concerned him. "It's not a huge upset. Why don't you repot your flower, and I'll run back out and get us something. Be back in a few," he said before grabbing keys from inside and getting in a truck she hadn't seen on the other side of the house.

"You made me bike there while you had a car?!" she shouted as he pulled out of the property.

"I figured you could use some time outside!" he called out with a laugh, and then he was gone. As she watched him disappear down the road, she sighed. He was right, after all.

Fallon brought her plant inside and inspected it. She traced her finger across every petal and leaf, down the stem, and into the soil. Flowers were Victoria's thing, not hers. She struggled to keep things alive, while Victoria could revive anything just by *looking* at it. Determined not to waste her new gift, she wandered outside, looking for a safe place to plant it. She debated keeping it inside, but remembered Victoria's outdoor garden and figured she would try that too. The animals mooed and baaed as they brushed against her, but she kept walking past the farm, convinced one of them would eat the flower if they had the chance.

After a few minutes, she stumbled across a field of thriving plant life. The last moments of the day washed the clearing in warm light, with colorful flowers and tall, billowing trees that led to a flowing river; it took her breath away. She stopped moving, soaking in the still beauty, when she heard a faint cooing sound. She looked around for its source, turning in every direction to look near the trees, and saw a small white bird perched on a low-lying branch not too far from her. She approached it slowly, not wanting to startle it. It watched her curiously.

"Well, hello, dove," her throat bobbed as she said the word.

Fallon decided to carve out a spot near the tree for her Holy Ghost orchid. Something told her it would thrive there.

She carefully removed the block of soil from the pot and placed it into the ground before scooting the dug-up pile of dirt back over it with her hands. When she finished and clapped the dirt off her fingers, the dove cooed again, calling Fallon over to it.

"What are you doing out here alone, huh?" Fallon tilted her head and smiled when the bird mimicked her. It didn't fly away when Fallon extended her pointer finger like she expected—it stepped from the branch to her finger, flapping its wings to readjust. "Aren't you pretty?" she thought out loud.

The bird blinked slowly, and inched its head closer to her. "Is this your home?" Fallon asked while looking over the field of tall flowers. "It reminds me of my own," she told the dove, her voice fading at the thought of the gardens in the courtyard. "Take care of this place, will you? I'll never see mine again," she finally said. It was something she knew, but hadn't come to terms with in the week she had been gone. She raised her hand to the branch and let the dove step back onto the bark. "Thank you," she said.

She didn't return to the farm until sunset. Emil hadn't gone looking for her, which she appreciated. Although he didn't know her situation, he had seen his fair share of dark days before, and after, August. If there was anyone who knew that understanding your emotions took time, it was him.

12

"**S**TAY UP LATE AGAIN, Victoria?"

Her head snapped to look at the source of the voice. She wiped the drool from her cheek with her forearm and smoothed her hair as her cheeks turned red. "Yes, sorry." Victoria scrambled to find the paintbrush she had last used, picking up the closest one to her and scribbling onto the cloud she fell asleep on. A mess of pink bled onto blue, ruining the shading she had spent hours blending out. She groaned and put the paintbrush back down.

Cressida, a fellow painter, flew around the patch of cloud that separated them and put her stool next to Victoria's. "You've been a little off lately. Is everything okay?"

Victoria sighed, exhausted. "No. I miss Fallon," she confessed.

Cressida's face twisted. "Why?"

Shocked, Victoria gasped softly. "Because she's my best friend? Everyone has either pretended they never knew her or ignored her disappearance completely. It's been weighing on me."

"I'm not surprised, Victoria. Given what she did, I'd say we're all better off without her."

Victoria's mouth hung open. "I can't believe you would say that to me. You know how close we were," she croaked. "And now that she's been accused of something, everyone turns their backs on her. It isn't fair," she decided as she dropped her paintbrush on her worktable.

"From what I heard, the seraphim did us a favor. Committing blasphemy is a serious offense; it's abhorrent. Frankly, I'm surprised you'd even speak her name." Cressida's voice was cold.

"Fallon is your friend too, Cressida." Victoria's jaw clenched while her knuckles turned white at her sides.

"*Was.*" She looked over her shoulder quickly. "Don't say that too loudly, I don't need an archangel breathing down my neck." Cressida sighed. "I can't believe it, looking back. Although something did seem a bit...off about her."

Victoria's neck craned in disgust. "*Off*? What was off about her, exactly?"

Cressida's confidence wavered when pushed. "You know, her...painting."

"Her clouds were always incredible, and you know it. She was a magnificent artist and did a lot of heavy lifting for this farm." She didn't mean for her voice to crack. Fallon was passionate about her work, and Victoria always admired how she could pour herself into her art.

"Maybe so, but her choice of colors was questionable. She was too loose with her creativity, and it finally caught up to her."

Victoria's nostrils flared as she processed Cressida's words. "You're being ridiculous. You know her, there's nothing wrong with her. She's a good person—"

"Then why would the seraphim say otherwise?" she blurted out, eyes wide.

Victoria sighed. "I don't know, Cressida. I truly don't."

Cressida gave her a knowing look. "I find that hard to believe; you two spent every minute together." She nearly rolled her eyes at the idea.

"And? We're close."

"Oh, we know. It was impossible not to notice, always giggling and sleeping at each other's homes. I'm surprised it wasn't carved out sooner." Cressida began to blend out the mistake Victoria made, swirling her brush until the blue and pink connected with the rest of the color story. "Don't let your bad judgment ruin your life here, Victoria. You can learn from her mistakes. Don't lose sight of what's important, okay?" She clamped her hand on Victoria's shoulder, who did her best not to flinch away.

With a tight-lipped smile, she nodded stiffly. "Got it. Thank you."

"Glad I could help," she grinned before flying back to her work station.

On edge, Victoria barely made any progress the rest of her workday. She went through the same motions that she had every day that week: flying home, changing clothes, and waiting until sundown.

She used to watch every sunset with Fallon. Without her around, the beauty in it was gone. The colors weren't as vibrant, and the view was disappointing. Once the lackluster sky turned, she crept back to the seraphim building and continued to look for clues. She wasn't sure how much longer she could sneak around before being caught or, worse, giving up.

Fallon needed her; she had to find her so they could clear her name, and go back to the way things were. Victoria liked their life together; it was safe and comfortable and happy, and she was determined to fix it.

When night fell on her conversation with Cressida, she had a new fire beneath her. If she doubted Fallon's innocence, that meant more people knew about Fallon than Victoria initially thought. The pit in her stomach continued to grow as she climbed through her usual window and made her way through endless pages of writing that didn't get her closer to Fallon.

Every night, she stood in front of the doors to the Seraphim Historical Library. No angels were permitted inside, which bothered Victoria. Information was freely shared among the angels; they didn't keep secrets. Victoria had to get inside, yet she couldn't make herself pick the lock. Night after night, she turned the handle and, when it didn't budge, retreated to a safer option. A less *helpful* option. A part of her knew that what she needed was in some old text on a shelf tucked away, but she couldn't force herself inside. She would find another way. At least, that's what she told herself.

Just as she was debating which office to rifle through next, she heard the unmistakable sound of a squeaky hinge. None of the doors she had used made a sound, including the entrances she'd been paraded through when Fallon was taken away. She froze to listen closer before hurriedly putting files in their right places. She slowly opened the office door and peeked into the hall. In the darkness, across the building, she saw a flash of white.

Victoria had snuck in several days in a row, and *no one* had come into the building after dark. So, she did what her heart told her to do.

She followed them.

Before she could second-guess her decision, she closed the door behind her soundlessly and flew toward the hall the angel had disappeared down, making sure to keep close to the walls. Only one door had light shining from the cracks. She put her ear to it and tried to slow her racing heart, but heard no voices, no signs of life. With her newfound adrenaline, she twisted the handle and poked her head inside.

No one.

She sighed and turned around to leave when she heard another crack somewhere behind a wall. Her brows pinched as she waited for another sound to give away their whereabouts. The next was further away, which confused her even further. She began to move every piece of furniture in the room, looking for some kind of passage. She hadn't been that far behind the mystery angel, she thought. Frustrated, she looked behind the bookcase and lifted the rug. When she found nothing, she felt silly. She was exhausted, after all. Perhaps she imagined it.

Victoria groaned before checking one last place: the framed picture on the wall. To her astonishment, it slid easily. She gasped and pushed it all the way to the side, revealing a massive hole in the stone; a tunnel.

"Good Heavens..."

She looked around the room, tucked her wings in close, and began to crawl through the tunnel toward her sure dismay. She trudged for several minutes before she arrived at the other side. When she was back on her feet, another crack sounded. She jumped, sure that she had been thwarted.

"Victoria?"

She squinted, sure she was mistaken. "Theo?" Why was the cloud farm archangel in the building after dark?

Hazel eyes stared back at her as he ran a hand through his blonde curls, attempting to look nonchalant. "What are you doing here?" he asked as he moved his hands behind his back.

Victoria crossed her arms. "I could ask the same of you."

Theo squinted back at her and shifted. "I asked you first." Victoria caught a glimpse of something in his hands and glanced down, leaning to the side to get a better look. He turned to keep her from seeing, but she jerked back and snatched what he was hiding.

"Don't! Victoria, please...give that back." His hands were clasped in front of him, pleading.

"Why, what is it?" She turned it over and realized it was a book. The cover read *Heavenly Travel*. She cocked a brow. "Planning a trip?"

"Victoria, I mean it, *please* give me the book." He reached for it, and she whipped her arm behind her, fully extended. Empty-handed, he sighed. "Not that it's any of your business, but, yes, I'm planning a trip."

Victoria scoffed. "All this for a travel guide?" She opened the cover to reveal the table of contents. "You could just ask the seraphim for recommendations, you know. They'd probably give you a whole list of—"

That's when she saw it. Section XII: Transportation between realms.

Her breath caught, and she slowly looked up at Theo. "I need this."

He shook his head. "No way, I found it first. Go find something else to read."

"You don't understand, I-I've been looking for ways to contact Fallon, and this might be exactly what I need!" Victoria felt hope for the first time in two weeks.

He looked sorry for her. "That's impossible, Victoria. The seraphim sent her away. There's no going back."

Victoria's heart wrenched. "You don't get it!" Her breaths came out shallow. She bit her lip to stop herself from getting emotional, but only managed to make herself bleed. "She was accused of—," her eyes traced the intricate crown molding as she put the words together and took a steadying breath. "They think she was in love with another angel." She met Theo's eyes, who looked far too understanding. "They think she was in love with *me*."

Theo nodded slowly as he walked to a white bench at the end of a wall of bookshelves. He patted the spot next to him and waited until Victoria sat down.

"I need to leave this place, Victoria." He looked at her with fear and sorrow in his eyes. "I can't wait for them to weed me out. I know it's coming, and I can't think about anything else. I'm jumpy, I can hardly sleep, I can't feel anything but paranoia."

Victoria let his confession settle. "Wait, you..." She couldn't find the right words.

"Yep," he answered, popping his lips. He leaned back against the flat wall of the bookshelf and slouched. "Which means it isn't safe for me here. I need *that*," he pointed at the book, "to leave. I have no other choice. If I don't do it myself, they'll do it for me and I'll be humiliated like—"

He stopped himself before saying Fallon's name, but Victoria's head fell anyway.

"I can't imagine what they did to her."

Theo's thumbs fiddled mindlessly. "I can. I've been imagining every possibility to prepare for the worst."

Victoria leaned back to put her head against the bookshelf. "This isn't fair. This is supposed to be the safest, happiest place in existence. But lately it feels," she searched for the right word. "Scary. It shouldn't be scary, right?"

Theo wiped his nose. "I don't think so."

Her lip quivered as tears filled her eyes. "I miss her so much," she muttered as one fell down her cheek.

He nodded, contemplating. "I know." After a moment, he held out his hand. "Let me look through the book. I'll comb through it, and I'll try to find answers for both of us." Victoria hadn't stopped crying, so he put a hand on her shoulder. "You'll find her."

She met his gaze without wiping her eyes, content with crumbling in front of someone who understood. "You think?"

"I really hope so," he shrugged. "For both of us."

13

"A LITTLE TO THE left."

Emil adjusted the frame.

"Too far."

"My shoulders hurt, I'm leaving it," he grunted as he walked to the other side of the room. "Look at that!" His hands clapped down on his dark wash jeans. "It looks great. Good pick, kid."

Fallon's shoulders lifted with pride. "Tak."

Emil chuckled, eyeing her from across the room. "Well, look at you! Learning things."

"I'm trying." The corner of her mouth lifted in a half-effort smile.

Emil snapped his fingers, his eyes widening. "Don't let me forget, this afternoon we need to use up the rest of those eggs. I don't need more chickens, so turn them into something." Emil pulled out a collection of random ingredients from the cupboard.

Fallon stood and pondered what she could come up with. "I haven't baked since..." She couldn't finish the thought.

Emil knew better than to pry. "It's been a while, huh? So, I get to be your guinea pig. Great." He made quick work of the dishes they'd dirtied and pulled his boots on. "I'll be outside if you need anything. Make anything you'd like, I'm not a picky eater," he chuckled as he patted his stomach.

Alone in the kitchen, Fallon bent over the counter and rested her head on her arms. What could she bake that she hadn't made in Heaven a million times before? No recipe in her mind wasn't consumed by Victoria, nothing she'd made wasn't praised by her dearest friend. What could she bake that didn't smell like Victoria's hair after an evening at Fallon's house?

She'd have to adjust eventually; living her life for a woman she'd never see again wasn't healthy. She tried to give herself grace; it had barely been a month since she was thrown from Heaven; moving on would take time. And yet, moving on from someone who had shaped her as a person felt *wrong*. Fallon felt that she owed it to Victoria to never forget her. If she was being honest with herself, she couldn't if she tried. Every flower on the side of the road whispered her name. The sun peaking through the clouds was a painful reminder of her existence. And then there was her newest prize, the dove orchid. An obvious, small dove sat in the center of the flower, its white petals a soft halo. She couldn't look at it without its beauty calling to Victoria's, couldn't touch its velvet petals and not think of grazing Victoria's skin in passing. Without her around, the world lacked color. The sunsets did, too.

No sunset looked the same from beneath the clouds.

Eventually, she decided to embrace her pain instead of hiding from it. She rifled through Emil's cabinets until she gathered every item from her mental list that he hadn't already brought out.

Flour, sugar, and salt melded with warm milk and butter before she cracked a few of the eggs from the farm. She mixed her dough and kneaded it until her wrists were sore and a thin layer of flour coated her forearms. For the filling, she whisked more butter with brown sugar and cinnamon—two of her favorite warm flavors.

Rolling the dough was more difficult without her usual array of colorful and carefully chosen baking supplies. Her kitchen in Heaven was carefully organized, with every utensil in a specific place. The order she created lifted a weight off her chest; a piece of her life she had complete control over. There, in Emil's kitchen, she managed. Despite the disarray and lack of tidiness, she became lost in the routine of baking. She coated the dough with the cinnamon filling, rolled and arranged them in a glass dish before placing them in the oven.

As she set 20-minute timer, Emil stepped inside and inhaled deeply. "It smells good in here, kid."

"Thanks," she called over her shoulder while whipping the icing together.

Emil stepped up next to her, squinting. "I had cream cheese?"

Fallon shook her head. "No, I had to make some myself with milk, vinegar, and salt."

"Huh." He looked at her inquisitively. "Where'd you learn this stuff?"

She shrugged. "I used to bake a lot with a dear friend of mine. She has a garden, and we would decorate whatever I made with her herbs or flowers. This," she said, pointing to the tray of cinnamon buns, "was her most common request. I've made it so many times, I could make it in my sleep." She didn't mention the fact that it was the dessert Victoria made on her birthday. Emil stuck his finger in the icing, and Fallon swatted his arm. "Hey, I need that!"

"You can always make more," he said after swiping another finger in the bowl.

She couldn't do anything but laugh—Victoria often did the same thing. She always joked that Victoria didn't like the cinnamon buns; she only wanted the frosting. It didn't bother her, though; Fallon would have made a million batches of frosting if it made Victoria happy.

"—all sticky."

Fallon looked at Emil with wide eyes, blinking.

"You didn't hear a thing I just said, did you?"

She brought her lips into her mouth and shook her head.

"What's bothering you, kid?" he asked with a worried brow.

Fallon grabbed a spatula and scraped the sides of the bowl. "Nothing, why do you ask?"

He crossed his arms over his chest. "You do that when you're lost in thought. I've seen you do it before." He poked her forehead with the hand not tacky from icing. "You've got something stirring up here."

Fallon put the spatula down on the counter. "I was in a bad place when I...left home. I guess I've been thinking about it a lot."

"Does this have anything to do with that friend you mentioned?"

Fallon's lips pulled up at the mention of her dove. "It has everything to do with her."

Emil looked at the timer and then out at the farm. "We've got some time before the animals need to be fed, and those come out of the oven. I think it's time we talk."

Fallon chewed at her lip, but nodded. "Okay." She followed him out to the field, and they sat on the grass.

Emil looked out over the pasture, wading in the heavy silence before he finally spoke. "August and I met when I was 29 years old. I had broken off an engagement 3 months before." When Fallon raised an eyebrow, he explained, "I hadn't been feeling like myself." He shrugged one shoulder. "I started having doubts about getting married, which, as I'm sure you can imagine, broke a few hearts." He chuckled, dryly. "My mother asked if Laurel did anything to hurt me, and I had to tell her no—that something else had come up. I didn't know how to explain to her that for two and a half years of my life, I had been playing pretend."

Fallon leaned forward, her mind focused.

"I stopped going out with my friends. I became a recluse who didn't leave my house unless I needed to prove that I wasn't dead."

She let him speak uninterrupted and without eye contact. She wasn't sure how long it had been since he told someone this story, and she knew better than to derail him.

"My mother begged me for months to go to a Sunday market with her. The idea made me want to rip my hair out, but...I started to realize how old she was getting. Her movements were slow, and her skin was so thin. I didn't know how much time she had left, so I finally agreed. It was horrible out that day," he laughed. "Gloomy and wet; the second I stepped out my door, I debated canceling, but something told me to follow through.

We were walking through the aisles of stalls when I looked across rows of jars on a table and saw the most *interesting* man. He had dark blonde hair that fell over the left side of his forehead, and a moustache I was jealous of. He had this—", he squinted like he could see it in the distance "—red and brown paisley button-down on, and brown pants. I swear, he let me try every single thing at the table, and watched my face while I did. A jar of jam wasn't the only thing I brought home from the market that day," he said.

Fallon gasped. "Emil!" she said through a laugh.

He put his hands up in defense. "What? He gave me a business card." Fallon rolled her eyes. "He told me to come by the shop sometime, and we couldn't get rid of each other after that. The next time I thought about marriage, it felt right. I wasn't scared about the future or worried that I was making the wrong decision." He smiled. "My mother was able to see me happy again. I know that gave her some peace when she passed."

Fallon sat in his confession. "I'm sorry about their passing."

Emil sighed softly, but remained smiling. "Me too, kid. Me too." When Fallon didn't reply, he looked at her. "It's only fair if you share something too, you know."

Fallon looked to the sky and shook her head. "I don't even know that there's a story to tell. I made my decisions and suffered the consequences."

Emil sat upright with a stern face. "If you're talking about whatever happened to your back when I found you, that isn't a consequence, Fallon. That's torture." When she didn't reply, he gently laid his hand on her forearm. "Please tell me that you know that."

She finally looked at him and felt the urge to tell him everything: her home in heaven, her place in the clouds, and how she lost it all. Victoria seemed like a larger-than-life topic, someone she could only discuss when she was ready to accept her fall from grace.

"I guess I'll start from the beginning."

Fallon recounted the day she met Victoria. She described the white lace shawl that draped Victoria's shoulders, the way her long brown hair had stray pieces falling out of its braid. A smile crept onto her face as she relived their adventures; she could almost hear the rushing water from the river they frequented. Every memory she shared with him caressed her heart, breathing life back into it.

"It sounds like you two mean a lot to each other," Emil tried when Fallon had gone silent.

She sniffled as she prepared herself for the next part of their story.

"I lived in a very strict town. One day, at work, I was pulled aside. Our—" she paused, "—overseers...had been watching us. They weren't pleased with the amount of time we spent together, or how we spent it. Their issue was with me, primarily." Fallon rubbed the top of her thighs to calm herself before digging crescent moons into the skin with her nails. "I was questioned about the nature of our relationship. They decided I wasn't being truthful, so they kept us apart." Her sniffling broke her thoughts into palatable pieces.

"And they did that to you?" Emil's throat bobbed. She couldn't bear to look at him, to see the emotion on his face.

She nodded, noiselessly, chewing at the inside of her cheek. Fallon pulled her knees to her chest to keep her composure.

Emil put his arm around her shoulder and pulled her into his side. "I'm so sorry, dear."

Fallon felt his chest heave as he cried, holding her together as she slowly fell further and further apart. She couldn't form the words; she couldn't describe how it felt to have a piece of herself stripped away. She wasn't sure how to tell him all that she had lost. For the time being, they had shared plenty. Any further probing could wait.

14

T HREE BOOMING KNOCKS WOKE Victoria before the sun rose. She looked around her dark bedroom, her flower-shaped fan churning the curtains, and rolled out from under her frilled bedsheets. Her heart jumped to her throat when she looked through her window and saw Theo waving on the other side.

Victoria turned the latch and pulled the window up. "I have a door," she pointed out, startled.

"I'm not taking any chances. If they stalked Fallon, they could be stalking us, too."

Her brows pulled. "If they were, we'd have been chastised by now."

Theo shrugged. "Maybe not. I don't understand them anymore; their reasons are their own. Who knows why they do things?"

Victoria nodded and perched on the edge of her bed. She pulled her knees up to her chest and wrapped her arms around them, motioning for Theo to sit on the pouf chair beside her standing mirror. "Did you find something?"

"I think so," he said with an unsure smile and plopped the book on his lap. He trailed his finger along its side, fluttering through the various colored tabs sticking out, before opening the book. "This," he pointed at a header. *Pons Memoriae.*"

Victoria stared at him, her eyes searching. "It locates memories?"

Theo shook his head. "It *uses* them. If you have a powerful enough memory, you can use it to find the person it's connected to." His knee bounced erratically, unable to contain his excitement. "From my reading, it would create a bridge between planes to the object or person you focus on." He looked at her, hopeful. "You could use this to find where Fallon is in Denmark. It could lead you right to her!"

Victoria jumped up from her bed and spun excitedly in the air. "This is it!" She landed on her fuzzy blue rug, grinning widely. "I need to think. Actually, I need to remember." Her hand flew to her head, clutching her hair at the roots as she thought. "We have so many happy ones, this could take me a while. I could pick one of our sleepovers, those always made my heart full. Or I could pick something more tender, like our trip to Sunset Lake." She had started pacing, flying in a low, repetitive circle, when a hand appeared in front of her. Theo waved it to bring her attention back to the book.

"It can't just be a happy one." His hand went to her shoulder, lightly guiding her feet back to the floor. "That may help you find her, but it won't lead you to her. What good would it do to know where she is with no way to get there? It needs to be a *powerful* memory. Something that consumes you or dominates any other thought; it needs to be a memory that altered your mind, or how you view life."

Victoria pouted before letting out a light scoff. "Okay, well...that may take a little more time. We've had a million moments together!" Her hands opened toward the sky, desperate. "How am I supposed to know which ones *changed* me as a being?"

Theo sat on her bed and cocked an eyebrow at her. "You really can't remember one time that Fallon may have made an impact on you?"

"Fallon affected everything I did." She sat back down with a huff. "My garden thrived after I met her; flowers seemed to bloom quicker. Rain didn't drown the buds—they thrived." She paused and started again. "She's a part of everything I am." Victoria looked down at her unkept nails. The remnants of polish held on by a thread, grown out to the very tip. She still couldn't bear to remove the last manicure Fallon gave her—their matching color.

Theo stared at her. "How long have you been in love with her?"

Victoria snapped to look at him, her mouth open. "I—I don't—"

Theo put his hands up in defense. "You don't have to explain anything to me, Victoria. Remember how we found each other," he reminds her while holding up the book. "As long as *you* know your heart, it should work."

She bit her lip and nodded. "I trust you."

He scoffed. "I hope so. I'm putting myself in the line of fire to help you, here."

"Aren't you helping yourself, too?" Victoria squinted at him, her head tilted.

"Shh, shh." He put an arm around her and rested his head on hers. "We're not talking about me right now."

It made Victoria smile, despite the turmoil taking place inside her head. "Thank you for reading through all that. I know you have your own problems to worry about, and it means a lot that you would help me."

"I want to see you succeed. I like you guys; Fallon was always kind to me." He let out a sigh. "It'll give me hope for myself if you manage to get out of here."

Victoria turned to look up at him. "Are we your test subjects?"

"Oh, definitely." He gave her a squeeze, and stood with the book. "I'll try to look through this some more at work later in my office. If I find something huge, you'll get called away. I hope you're okay with that," he told her as he opened the window he came through.

"Fine by me," she confessed. "Everything I've painted lately has *sucked*."

"Hmm. I wonder why that is..." He threw her a knowing glance and went back out into the barely lit morning.

She wasn't going to get any more sleep, too distracted by her new mission. She sat at her vanity, running a brush through the same section of hair until she finally came to. With no one but herself around to hear, she rambled. "She's your friend. You have happy memories with her. That's normal." Her delicate fingers separated her hair and braided it over her shoulder. "You haven't done anything wrong." She froze, and eyed herself in the mirror. "You haven't done anything wrong."

Although she couldn't stomach the idea of breakfast, she made herself eat a snack before going to the cloud farm. She didn't want to be nauseous *and* lost in thought. After putting on her apron, Victoria gathered her color choices for the day and got right to work. If she stayed busy, no one would notice her staring into the void.

She started with a soft pink, fully saturating the cloud. Upon looking at it, she decided it needed a deeper hue to balance it out. A darker pinkish purple melted seamlessly into the base color, but it was still missing something. Victoria swiped her paintbrush through the bowl of purple and lost herself. It looked beautiful; *almost* perfect, yet somehow still missing something. She kept swirling her brush, blending the edges until they disappeared entirely. Someone laughed a few rows over, completely unaware of her, and she startled back into the present moment. The purple had gotten so saturated that it looked stormy.

Victoria decided she liked it.

Pastels and vibrant, lively colors dominated the sky. What rule dictated that the clouds couldn't have more depth?

Victoria flew back to the array of shades and filled her arms with colors she used to think were *bad*.

Red was sensual. Blue was a *morning* color. Green was hungry and greedy. Victoria loved those colors; nothing was wrong with them.

She found an empty cloud and began flinging paint onto it. Blue crashed into yellow and pink and when that started to look muddy, she flew over the cloud to the other side and covered it with green, orange, and purple. It was the worst thing she had ever made, but it was *fun*. At a certain point, she stopped cleaning her brush between colors. Each bowl had been kissed by a random color, each of them slowly turning to brown in their pools. Victoria giggled as she made long, sure strokes overlapping one another.

Someone cleared their throat behind her. She turned, expecting to see Theo, when her smile quickly dropped.

"What is this?" Dimitri clipped with a stern expression.

Victoria put the paintbrush behind her ear without wiping the paint off. "It's called *expression*. Isn't it wonderful? I thought to myself, 'You know what sounds fun? Making a hodgepodge.' So, that's what I did." She planted her hands firmly on her hips.

The snarky smile he gave her was void of joy. "I'm glad you're having fun. But we have to scrap this, I can't use it," he said as he waved toward the cloud. Two male archangels flew over and started to lift it from her station.

"You can't do that, I made this!" She pushed the cloud back down, struggling against their strength.

Confusion coated his face, mixed with something like disgust. "I know you did, and we can't use it. That isn't going in the sky, Victoria. You know better than this." His chin dipped. "I expect more from you."

She dropped her arms and stuttered, thinking of a rebuttal. When the cloud was four feet above her station, she called out, "Wait!" They halted, and she looked to Dimitri. "Let me keep it."

"You can't keep a cloud, Victoria, that's ridiculous." He began to shoo them away, but Victoria flew in front of them.

"Why not? It won't hurt anyone. I made it, and you don't want it. You don't have to destroy it, just...let me take it home."

Dimitri rolled his eyes and scoffed. "Okay, fine." He flew up to meet her eye level. "I don't know what your goal is, here, but you need to rein it in. This was a waste of time."

She stayed there while he and the two archangels flew back toward the seraphim building. When she collected her thoughts, she looked at her messy, muddy cloud and smiled. She felt a creative spark for the first time since Fallon left.

Her face twisted as she continued looking at it. Fallon didn't leave, she thought to herself.

Fallon was taken from her.

Victoria remembered the tears in her eyes when she said goodbye in that cell. When she managed to sleep, she didn't dream anymore; she saw Fallon's puffy, red eyes.

She didn't need to be reminded of her conversation with Theo; it had burned into her brain.

How long have you been in love with her?

Theo didn't know what he was talking about. Just because they had the same mission didn't mean their motivations were the same. She still hadn't fully processed why Fallon was thrown from the clouds; she hadn't let herself come to terms with her best friend wanting more from their relationship. Things between them were perfect; they both had someone to confide in and lean on, someone they could be themselves around.

Victoria couldn't deny she thought about Fallon.

She would wake up ready to start the day, knowing she would see Fallon at work. She made sure her hair was perfect before going over to watch the sunset. She loved planning their outings to the park and cooking together; she just loved *her.*

A chill went down her spine. She needed to unpack that, and quickly.

As soon as her shift was over, she looked for Theo. He was in his office, and his eyes grew wide when she turned the corner. He shook his head quickly and mouthed *Not here.* Victoria held up eight fingers and pointed to herself, hoping he would understand. He kicked his chin toward the door as a sign for her to leave.

She had to remember not to take it personally. Theo liked her and, hopefully, he trusted her. He was right, they couldn't risk speaking where someone might hear them. So, she waited anxiously for him to arrive at her home. Before the sun set, she picked every weed out of her garden and scrubbed her counters so intensely that Fallon could knead dough on them.

She had gone into such a cleaning frenzy that she hadn't noticed the sun go down. When Theo came through her bedroom window and walked into her living room, her hand flew to her mouth to stifle a scream.

"Don't *do* that!" she wheezed through rapid breaths.

Theo looked at her, astounded, his hands up defensively. "You *told* me to come here!"

She grabbed his arm and pulled him down onto the couch next to her. Her face was stern, and her voice was quiet. "How did you...know? You know, that you felt..."

Theo chuckled. He felt for her, knowing how difficult it was for him to understand on his own. "It was a bit more obvious for me. I appreciate a pretty girl, don't get me wrong. But, they've never sung to me the way a male's angled features do. Something about them is rugged in such a beautiful way that I can't help but stare." His brows dipped, his soul bare.

Victoria nodded slowly, then inclined her head. "I don't feel that way."

He smiled at her. Not in a way that made her feel silly, but it made her feel heard. "It's not the same for everyone, Victoria. Your feelings will be different because they're your own. And, it may take a while for you to understand them and recognize them." Theo leaned in and bumped her shoulder with his. "It'll be alright. I know this is a lot, but you'll get through it."

Victoria wrapped her arms around his middle. "So will you."

15

FALLON LOOKED DOWN AT the container of wriggling worms. "I am *not* putting my hand in there."

Emil pulled the slack out of his line. "You won't catch anything if you don't."

She shrugged. "I'm fine with that," she said, and turned to walk back toward the truck, its yellow paint rusted at the high points.

"We're not going home until you get one!"

Fallon in her tracks. "What if I never catch one? You won't sit out here all night."

Emil cocked a brow. "Wanna bet, kid?"

She groaned, but went back to the lake and picked up the other rod. "This is inhumane."

"It's the circle of life. I promise you, the fish you catch has eaten lots of other, smaller fish."

"I still don't like it."

"I know, kid. It's called empathy. It's a good thing to have, but it can make life hard." Emil stuck his pole in the dirt and sat next to it.

Fallon looked down at him, her arms holding the pole further out than necessary. "You don't even have to hold it?"

"I know what cues to look for. I've been fishing since before you were born."

Fallon's brows rose; she wasn't sure about that. Then, her arms were yanked forward. She looked to Emil, who had a boyish grin and wrinkled eyes. "What do I do?!"

Emil stood and tried to coach her. "Pull the rod up, and twist the handle on the side." When she did, he said, "Okay, now stop twisting and let it go out a little."

"Let it go? Won't I lose it?" She thought he truly might want to stay out here all night.

Emil shook his head. "It needs room so it doesn't freak out. Start reeling again," he pointed at the pole.

Fallon reeled as fast as she could until a trout appeared above the water. "Look at me!" She put the handle of the pole on the ground and grabbed the fish with her bare hand. The brown-silver fish was sticky in her palm. "This is disgusting." She removed her hand and held it out with her palm facing the sky.

Emil couldn't help but laugh. "You weren't supposed to grab it like that," he explained as he grabbed a massive pair of pliers and hooked them onto the trout's mouth. He handed the plier-held fish to Fallon, who still kept it at arm's length, and pulled out a camera. "What do you call a fish with no eyes?"

Fallon's mouth fell open, and she groaned. "Ew, why would I know that?"

Emil held the camera up to his eye and yelled, "Fsh!" Fallon's look of disgust was briefly overthrown by amusement as she held the fish out in front of her, and Emil pressed the shutter button. "We'll get that developed. It'll look good on the wall," he decided as he took the fish from her.

"You're putting me on the wall?" She dipped her hands in the water to get the fish slime off and wiped them on a rag she now kept tied to her belt loop. She looked at Emil, who was sitting on a flipped-over bucket with a knife to the fish's head.

"If you're squeamish, look away," he said jokingly. Fallon listened and jerked her head at just the right moment, but she heard him cut the fish. "Of course you're going on the wall." Ice moved when he put the headless fish in the cooler, and he looked up at her from his bucket stool. "We never got to have kids of our own, but...I think August would've really liked you."

Fallon gave a tight-lipped smile to keep herself from crying. "I would've loved to meet him."

Emil nodded with a matching expression. "I'd love to meet Victoria, you know."

Fallon stared out over the water. "I don't know if that's possible."

"*You* caught a fish. Anything is possible, kid," he said with a playful punch to the shoulder.

She sighed. "Yeah, well, I don't know if *I'll* ever even see her again."

"Ever is a bit dramatic, isn't it?"

Fallon gave a dry chuckle. "Not with this." He waited for her to explain. "When I was taken away, part of the deal was that if I confessed and left forever, they would leave her alone. That's why I'm here," she explained with a shrug.

Emil braced his hands on his knees. "You left her so she'd be safe." When Fallon nodded, he sighed. "*That's* love."

"Yeah." Fallon looked down at her hands.

"People are a lot like fish."

Fallon slowly turned to look at him. "Are they?"

He kept his eyes on the water. "You have to let them go sometimes, but they come back. If they're meant to."

Fallon nodded with pursed lips. "I'm not gonna get my hopes up." She picked up the cooler and walked it back to the truck, Emil not far behind her with his bucket and the fishing poles.

"Don't lose hope entirely. Things have a funny way of working out."

Every day that week, Fallon sat in the grove and watched her flower. The dove greeted her every time, its gentle coos soothing her nerves. After a busy morning taking care of the farm, she put her hands behind her head and leaned back on the soft grass, watching the forgotten dove soar delicately through the sky. Her orchid wasn't thriving when she brought it home, but lately it had started to show signs of improvement. The petals were full and bright, and pink spots had developed in the center. She learned a few things from Victoria in their time together; not enough to have a thriving garden, but she was determined to keep this flower alive. The grove she put it in was taking care of it, solidifying her thought that things didn't grow well when stifled.

Emil returned from Fern's and called out for Fallon to help bring in the animal feed. When she didn't respond, he found her in the grove with her head against the ground. "You alright?"

She stayed still. "Yeah."

"It won't grow with you staring at it like that." He sat next to her, content to sit outside.

Fallon sighed heavily through her nose. "It reminds me of Victoria," she said plainly.

"I see..." He stretched out on the grass next to her and stared into the tree dangling above them. "Why don't we get you into town for a little while? It's a beautiful day; you could use some socialization. And some sun..." He poked at her arm. "You're practically see-through."

Her head twisted, her face unamused. "Gee, thanks."

Emil slowly got up, grabbed her arm, and pulled her to her feet. "Come on, let's go."

"What about dinner?" she said, trying to prevent the inevitable.

"We'll have dinner out. Go," he said, pointing toward the truck.

Fallon put her hands up, giving in. "Okay, okay."

In the two-seater truck, Fallon's head rested against the window. Trees passed her by, full and green. Emil, with his hands at 10 and 2, felt the weight of the air inside the cab. He lingered at stop signs and took turns slowly, keeping her from tipping over and crumbling to the best of his ability. "You gonna be okay, kid?"

Fallon shrugged. "I guess so. It's silly, really; a plant shouldn't make me feel this way. Just because they share a name doesn't mean it should have this effect on me."

"I thought you said it was called a Perestara or something; a ghost plant." He adjusted his grip on the wheel, his hands clammy.

His butchered pronunciation made her smile, if only for a moment. "Holy ghost plant, yeah. Fern called it the dove." When Emil didn't ask another question, she looked at him. "I used to call Victoria that. Dove was my nickname for her," she told him.

"That's sweet." He turned his attention back to the road. "August and I had pet names, too."

Fallon peeked at him without moving her head from the window. "We were never together," she said quickly. "Not like...you two."

Emil mimicked her secretive stare. "I know you weren't. Names can be for friends, too." When Fallon's defenses retreated, he continued. "August called me Minsk. He thought he was being clever because *min skat* means treasure, but Minsk is also the capital of Belarus."

It made the corner of Fallon's mouth quirk. "I like that. It's cute," she fiddled with a strand of hair as she spoke.

"He thought so, too. He didn't like my name for *him*, though." He made himself laugh. "Trold."

Fallon's mouth opened. "Does that—"

"Yep." They looked at each other for one second before laughter filled the cab. "When we first started seeing each other, he would shower right before bed and sleep with wet hair. I thought it was odd, but he insisted he slept better. It looked that way, too; his hair stuck in every direction when he woke up."

In the wake of his story, Fallon felt a sense of calm. "Victoria's so...peaceful. Her voice is sweet and melodic. She's always so gentle." Fallon stared out the windshield. "She's always the first to offer help or compliment a stranger."

"She sounds like she'd be August's best friend."

"Yeah," she sighed. "She's mine, too."

Emil pulled into a parking spot on the street and turned off the car, but didn't move to get out. When Fallon pulled the handle on the door, he spoke. "Love is funny, you know."

She turned to him, tears already threatening to spill.

"You did a brave thing, Fallon. I know she thinks about you, even though you're gone. I know I would."

Fallon bit her lip, her chin quivering. "You think so?"

"Yeah, I do." Emil walked around the truck, opened her door, and gave her his hand. "Let's eat, søde."

She squinted, but didn't question it. "I didn't realize how hungry I was."

Emil chuckled. "I did. You start acting like a trold when you're hungry."

Fallon swatted at his hand and got out on her own. "Unbelievable."

16

"WHAT DO YOU MEAN we have two days?"

Victoria paced her room, barefoot, while Theo sat cross-legged on her bed with the book open in his lap.

"I've been doing the math; the Feast of Trumpets was seven days ago, which means the Day of Atonement happens in three more."

With a half-bitten nail in her mouth, she asked, "Why does that affect us? It happens every year." She ripped off the nail, pulling a bit of skin with her. "*Ouch.*"

Theo reached out and grabbed her wrist. "Stop biting your nails, or you'll rip them all off." He flipped the book closed and gave her a solemn look. "The Day of Atonement is all about cleansing impurities. I don't know about you, but the idea of confessing my sins to a seraph, given what we know, sounds like—"

"Don't say it," Victoria cut him off, her eyes closed to keep away the idea.

He sighed, stood from the bed, and put his hands on her shoulders. "It sounds like hell, Victoria."

"We don't have to confess every impure thought we've ever had, Theo. It's never been that severe," she whined while staring at her red, puffy cuticles.

"You think they'll accept a less-than-worthy confession from *us*? It's been two months since they took Fallon. I can almost guarantee I'm on a list somewhere of angels needing to be dealt with, and you're likely not far down!" His voice rose in a panic, the vein in his neck popping as his breath quickened.

Victoria looked stunned and took a step back. "You really think that?"

He closed his eyes, their situation weighing on him. "I won't risk being wrong. I need to leave, so you should get ready." Before Victoria could argue further, he picked up the book and went back through the window, leaving Victoria to fester in her thoughts.

Although she wasn't sure *what* to think.

Theo was her ticket to Fallon; she knew that. But what if he was wrong? What if the seraphim *didn't* have their sights set on them? They had time—time for her to make up her mind, to be sure, to breathe. Theo's plan meant relying on instinct, and Victoria wasn't sure she could trust hers.

What did she know?

She couldn't trust the seraphim.

Theo was scared.

Fallon loved her. *How*, she couldn't look at too closely...but she loved her.

And Victoria loved her too.

When Theo asked her the next day what her choice was, she put aside her fear, deciding that her friends were more important. He reminded her to pick a memory—a memory strong enough to build the bridge to Fallon.

"We'll meet at the pergola in the Garden of Michael. It's far enough away from the temple to be out of public view, but not so far that we look suspicious flying in that direction." Victoria nodded, still a bit unsure. Theo could read it on her face. He pulled her into a tight hug and held her there. "Thank you," he choked. "I wasn't sure you'd be ready," he said into her hair.

"Me neither," she said against his chest. When they pulled apart, she held his hands in the space between them. "But I won't keep you here any longer. You're right, it isn't safe."

He pushed her hair aside and cupped her face to force her eyes to his. "Don't do this for me, Vic. Do this for you. Do it for every moment you looked for Fallon after they took her. You *have* to find her."

She grabbed his wrist and nodded. "You're right. For Fallon."

Victoria didn't sleep a wink.

She lay in bed and stared at the ceiling, combing through every interaction she ever had with Fallon—every smile they shared, every conversation behind closed doors. She stayed awake the entire night to make sure that she *had it*. She couldn't fail Theo. All the work he put in over weeks of reading and planning led to her stepping up and making a choice. One she would make in just a few hours.

Every item in her closet was thrown onto her bed and floor. Picking an outfit had never been so complicated, but this was the outfit Fallon would see her in after so long without each other. She couldn't resist and decided on something in Fallon's favorite color: a light pink, billowy, long-sleeved top with a bow at her sternum, and ruffles on the bottom. She paired it with a calf-length green silk skirt, one with small purple flowers all over it. She wasn't sure how long she planned to stay; she hadn't thought about anything further than seeing Fallon, truthfully. Deciding to be better safe than sorry, she stuffed a bag with her favorite outfits and said *See you soon* to her cottage before flying off to meet Theo.

He sat on the pergola, his knee bouncing anxiously. "There you are!"

"You're early," she noted as she landed in front of him.

"Couldn't sleep," he said. The dullness of his hazel eyes proved it.

"You and me both." Her shoulders rose and fell heavily. "Are you ready?"

He nodded repeatedly. Slowly. "Ready as I'll ever be." He took her hand and walked her underneath the ivy-covered pergola. "I need you to picture it. Whatever memory you've decided on, you need to wipe everything from your mind until nothing but that remains." His voice was shaky. "Close your eyes."

She obeyed and took a steadying breath.

"What do you see?"

"I see Fallon asleep. Usually, we have sleepovers at her house, but this time I wanted her to come to mine. Her hair is messy, lying out all around her head with a few strands splayed over her neck. I reach out to move them, and she stirs. We stayed up late, and Fallon gets grumpy when she's tired, so I stroke her hair to calm her. I know that she's back to sleep, and yet—I can't help but keep touching her. I count every single freckle on her face, from her chin to her hairline. That's when I notice the cow lick at her right temple. My fingers are drawn to it, tracing over the short, soft hairs repeatedly. She looks so relaxed," she recounted with a smile. "She's never done well in crowds, always picking at her nails or twisting her hair; it makes her anxious. But now, she's calm. I close my eyes and wish she could feel this way forever. It hurts me that I can't ease her troubles. I want this to last as long as it can, so she can feel this way even for a little while. My shoulder finally starts to cramp when her eyes slowly flutter open. Crisp and blue, like a clear sky.

'Good morning, Fal.'"

When Victoria opened her eyes again, Theo nodded. "You deserve to be happy, Victoria."

Her voice cracked. "Thank you."

Theo targeted all of his energy into Victoria's memory—into her words. He spoke in a hushed, breathy voice. "Haec memoria ad me locum perveniat, quem videre non possum. Satis sit, sint omnia. Utere hac fenestra in animam meam, et recipe me in cor meum." As he spoke, a hazy lavender mist appeared next to them. By the time he finished, it was a dense, thick fog.

Victoria opened her eyes and cheered. "It worked!" She dropped his hands and jumped in place, trying to contain her excitement. "Theo, it worked!" Theo grunted as Victoria squeezed him tightly.

"Tell Fallon I said hello, will you?"

She nodded feverishly. "I will. I can't thank you enough." Victoria turned toward the purple fog cloud with her bag at her side and waved at Theo before visiting her friend.

But when she stepped toward it, she bounced off. Her face twisted as she tried again, this time putting her hand up to the cloud. She pushed harder, and still, her hand wouldn't penetrate the barrier. She looked at Theo, her forehead creased and her heart pounding. "What's happening? Why can't I go through?"

Theo hurriedly scanned the book with worried brows. Page after page, he frantically followed his finger looking for an answer, when his face dropped.

"What is it?" Victoria looked over his shoulder, trying to find what he saw.

"Angels can't exist on Earth."

Time froze. "That's impossible. Fallon is *there*, what do you mean angels can't—"

"Victoria."

"What!?" she cried. Theo looked at her with a piti-ful expression. "What happened to her, Theo?" Her heart dropped.

Victoria knew. She knew, but she couldn't fathom it being true.

"Fallon fell to Earth, which means...she doesn't have wings."

With a thud, Victoria fell to her knees. She stared at the swirling purple cloud. "Angels can't exist on Earth," she repeated in a whisper.

"The only way you can get to her is if..."

Her head jerked toward Theo as she reminded herself to breathe. "No..." Her throat bobbed.

He nodded. "I'm sorry, Victoria." He put a hand on her shoulder and squeezed, trying to offer any bit of comfort.

Victoria's eyes didn't stray. She heaved a trembling breath from her open mouth. "I have to see her."

Theo shook her shoulder. "You *can't*, Vic! Not with your wings."

She bit her lip. "I understand." Victoria stood slowly, her attention never moving from her wading future. Her arm traveled across her chest to her back, where she dug her fingers into her heavenly feathers.

"Victoria?"

"You have to grab the other one. I don't think I have the strength to do it on my own." Her voice was steadier. Her chest barely moved.

Theo pushed her shoulder, making her face him. "You don't have to do this, Vic, we can keep looking."

Just as he said that, they both heard the beating of wings—several pairs of them—and they knew what was coming.

She looked up at him. "I'm out of time, Theo." She yanked on her wing with every muscle she could command and screamed. The wings beat faster, closing in on their location. "Theo," she clipped, trying to turn his focus from the sky. "Pull!"

They heaved together, the scream that erupted from Victoria dispersing a cloud outside the pergola.

"Again!" she yelled at him. Victoria clawed at her back, but couldn't get a firm enough grip. She heard him sniffle, and his hold loosened. "Theo, please!"

He repositioned his hands at the base of her wings, his fingers brushing her shoulder blades, and he pulled. Theo rocked his body forward for momentum and sat back into his heels, separating the first half of the wing from her skin. Drops of blood fell on her white flats as a group of seraphim broke through the clouds, heading right for the pergola.

"Stop!" Dimitri's face was furious as his voice boomed in an echo. Four archangels that were almost twice his size flanked him in their descent.

"One more time!" she yelled through her tears. "1...2..."

Victoria leaned forward and pulled herself toward the marble column of the pergola at the same time Theo forced the already damaged skin from her body.

She turned slowly, the column supporting most of her weight. Theo's hands were soaked in red, shaking. She reached up and pulled him by his collar, further staining the shirt, to rest his forehead against hers. "Thank you," she croaked.

He shook his head violently. "You have to go. *Now.*" Theo pushed her toward the portal that had begun to shrink, its window growing smaller.

Before she could reach it, the archangels were on their feet, bounding into the pergola. Dimitri shoved Victoria to the ground, her body screeching as she fell on her arm.

"Don't you touch her!" Theo yelled. Two archangels held his arms behind his back as he struggled. Dimitri reached down toward Victoria and wrapped a lock of her hair around his finger. Theo kicked and thrashed, breaking one arm free from his captor. With his free hand, he punched the archangel's face with the back of his fist.

Dimitri turned his head from Victoria to shout, "Hold him!"

In an overlapping yell, Theo cried, "*Now*!" The other archangel was back on his feet, blood falling from his nose.

With the rest of her energy, Victoria sank her fingers into the purple void. As soon as they touched, she was gone.

Theo let out a cry of laughter from the ground while Dimitri planted a foot on his back. Seething, he flipped Theo over and punched him repeatedly. "What's so funny? You failed," he seethed.

Theo shook his head, the movement making him dizzy. He barely opened his swollen eyes and said, "She made it. That's all I cared about."

Dimitri scoffed. "I'm glad you're pleased with yourself. Enjoy that feeling," he said. "You'll never feel it again."

17

FALLON HANDED EMIL ANOTHER handful of weeds, now used to the feeling of dirt beneath her nails. "You really need to do this more often."

He shrugged with his bucket full of dirt. "But you do it so well," he whined.

Her hands froze midpluck as she slowly turned to him. "I pick weeds well?"

"My knees would be killing me right now. You probably feel fine, though, so full of youth."

Fallon shook her head with a laugh and went back to clearing the garden. A flash of light cut through the sea of tall grass, startling her, and she stood. "Did you see that?" she asked him, her fist full of stems and roots.

Emil put the bucket down and took off his hat to scratch his head. "I think so? No clue what it was, maybe someone nearby had farm equipment malfunction."

Fallon used her hand to shield the Sun from her eyes. "Hm. I'm gonna go check it out, see if someone dumped their trash. Some broken glass, maybe?" She brushed her hands on her jeans and marched through the field in the direction of the light. As she moved, she waved her hand through the ryegrass, keeping her eye out for any critters or obstacles.

A low moaning sound caused her to jump. She froze, standing painfully still, waiting to see if it happened again. When it didn't, she called out, "Hello?"

Silence.

"Is someone out here?" Nothing answered her, and she continued looking. Fallon had finally decided to give up and walk back to the garden when a portion of ryegrass shifted in her peripheral vision. There was something in the field, and she was going to find it.

She tried again. "This isn't funny!" The closer she got, the faster her heart beat. When she was steps away, she moved aside a wall of greenery and gasped. Then, she called for Emil. Fallon knelt in disbelief. By the time Emil arrived, she was in shock.

"What's goin' on? Did you find—" And then he saw her.

A brunette woman in a pink top and green floral skirt, lying on her back with her head in Fallon's lap.

"Is that who I think it is?" His voice was quiet, as if he could wake the, yet again, unconscious woman in his field.

With her quivering lip, Fallon nodded. She rocked back and forth as she touched Victoria's face; the rosiness that usually kissed her cheeks was absent. Her nose grazed Victoria's forehead as she dipped down to whisper, "What did you do, dove?"

Emil paced in a circle, scratching his head and stroking his curly, grey goatee. "We need to get her inside."

Fallon shook her head, frantic. "She's too pale. I can't move her, I-I don't know what they did to her." Her voice was thick with concern.

Emil planted his hand on the top of Fallon's head. "I took care of you when you showed up, didn't I? We can't keep a close eye on her if she's outside. We'll move her carefully, get her cleaned up and comfortable. Alright?" When she nodded, he motioned for her to slide out from underneath Victoria so he could pick her up.

"Let me help you." She looked up at him with pained, desperate eyes, and he took a step back. She moved to Victoria's legs and slid her hands between her skin and the warm grass. Emil carefully put his arms under Victoria's and lifted with Fallon. With a firm grip and unwavering determination, they walked her all the way to the house in one go. It was strange for Fallon—seeing Victoria unconscious on the same couch she had found herself on a few months ago.

Sunset came and went, and Fallon didn't leave her side.

"You'll be waitin' a while," Emil said from the kitchen doorway.

Fallon sat on the floor next to the couch with her knees pulled up to her chest, and her arms around her legs. "I know."

With a grunt, Emil sat down next to her. "You didn't move for two days. Even when you did, you wouldn't open your eyes. Couldn't, maybe."

"You never told me that," she said with a side glance.

He huffed out a laugh. "I was worried I dragged a dead girl into my house. Sat right there," he pointed to his red and tan striped armchair, "the whole night, making sure you didn't stop breathing."

Fallon chuckled before leaning her head against his shoulder, exhausted. "I need her to be okay."

"She will be. If she's even *half* as stubborn as you are, she'll be alright." Emil put an arm around her and squeezed. "I'll bring you a blanket." When he stood, Fallon grabbed his ankle.

"Thank you," she said.

He knew she wasn't talking about the blanket. "Any time, søde." He leaned down and kissed the crown of her head before bringing her the pillow and blanket from her room. "Let me know when you need me," he reminded her, and went off to bed.

Candlelight flickered over Victoria's barely rising chest. Fallon raked her eyes over every visible spot of skin, checking for any sign of injury. Scrapes, cuts—anything she could tend to while Victoria slept. Her knees looked fierce, with brown and purple bruises on both of them. Her elbow was banged up, too, and Fallon got angrier the longer she looked. She made a mental list of questions she had for Victoria when she woke. Wrapped in her blanket on the floor, she held Victoria's hand until her eyelids finally won in the battle of wills.

Crackling from the kitchen startled Fallon out of sleep. The curtains were drawn, but she could tell the sun was high. "Emil?" she groaned, her voice thick with sleep.

"In here," he called out. She went to him and found him dressed to tend the farm with a pan in his hand. "I know you're gonna say you're not hungry, but I don't care. You've gotta eat a little something."

She sighed, but agreed. "Can I eat in the living room?"

He nodded. "I thought you might say that. Be right back." Fallon watched as he went into the barn and came out with a wooden contraption. He walked it into the living room and opened up what looked like a tiny table. "I got into woodworking a long, long time ago. You can use this." Once he was sure Fallon would eat, he went back to work outside. The wind had been brutal the last few days, and he needed to prepare his crops for cooler weather. He still had a few weeks until he needed to worry about planning for lower temperatures, but knew it would take him a while to adjust, as it always did.

Fallon sat on the couch with her dinner tray, watching for the steady rise of Victoria's chest. If it faltered, even for a moment, she stopped chewing until it resumed. She put her empty plate on the counter and sat right back down, eyes trained. After several hours, Emil returned to the house to find her in the exact same spot. He sat down with a huff and put a hand on her shoulder.

"Why don't I give you a breather, hm? I'll sit here with her while you clean up. Take a shower, drink some water."

Fallon looked at him, unsure.

"I'll be right here the whole time," he assured her.

She nodded and decided it was for the best—she couldn't be helpful if she lost her mind.

"Just for a little while," she whispered before forcing herself to the bathroom. She lingered at the doorway, her fingers pressing into the wooden frame. After a few deep breaths, she closed the door and twisted the shower knob on the wall. While it heated, she pressed her back against the door and replayed the previous afternoon in her head.

Did the archangels send her as punishment?

That would imply Victoria broke the rules, which wasn't like her at all.

Fallon stood in the shower, motionless. Water fell on her like rain, sealing strands of hair to her face. She braced her arms against the shower wall and allowed herself to cry.

Having Victoria was supposed to be a *good* thing. But, not knowing why or how she arrived ate away at Fallon. Surely, they couldn't have made the same mistake. She made this sacrifice so that Victoria would be safe. Fallon had started to come to terms with her new reality. She had begun to accept losing everything: her home, her friends, a job that she loved, and the woman she sacrificed it all for.

She was never supposed to see her again, yet there she was. Unconscious in another room with bruises and scrapes on her legs and arms.

Victoria was going to be okay, Fallon decided. There was no other option.

18

"**A**RE YOU SURE IT'S alright if I go? I promise I won't be gone too long, I just need to stretch my legs and pick up a few things."

Fallon nodded and fiddled with her hair. "We'll be alright. You need to feel like a normal person. Take your time."

He gave a short, clipped nod. "Okay. You know how to get to town in case of an emergency?"

She let out a small, dry chuckle. "Yes, Emil, I know. I'll be fine."

He put his hand on her shoulder and squeezed. "Alright, kid. I'll see you in a little while." He grabbed his keys and stepped out the door. "I'll bring you back somethin'!" he yelled with a wave.

Fallon started to return his wave when the door shut, and she was alone with a still-sleeping Victoria. She had to repeatedly remind herself that *she* was out for a long while before she came to; Emil wouldn't let her forget.

"Give her time," he said over and over again.

"I'm trying," she always replied.

The first hour after Emil left, Fallon sat in her guilt. If she hadn't started all this, Victoria wouldn't be out cold with injuries in an unfamiliar plane. They would still be picking flowers and baking pastries while the sun set if she hadn't gone and ruined everything. Every time she looked at her still body, that was all she could think about.

After that hour of silence, she started to go mad. Being cooped up inside wasn't helping her spiraling thoughts or the weight of her decision. It would only be for a minute, she told herself, as she pulled on a light sweater and stepped outside with bare feet.

The cool grass against her anxiously warm skin was a welcome shock. The wind softly blew the knotted hairs away from her face as she stood with her arms crossed over her chest. She closed her eyes and soaked in the sound of rustling leaves and chittering birds as one of the smaller goats made its way to her and rubbed against her leg like a cat.

"How've you been, Shirl?" she asked as she pet the curly thing.

Shirley nipped at her pant leg, startling her. She chuckled, knowing that meant Shirley was hungry. "Okay, okay!" she told her as she filled the troughs nearby. "Are you happy now?" Shirley bleated at her in thanks and buried her head in the pile of food, despite other animals trying to push her aside.

Feeling rejuvenated, Fallon slowly made her way back to the house. She took a step through the front door and looked over at the couch that Victoria—

Wasn't on.

Fallon's heart stalled in her chest as she ran to the kitchen and found nothing. She opened every door and checked inside, but couldn't find her. She started to panic by the time she checked the bathroom, flinging the door open.

Behind it was Victoria, with her arms behind her head, pulling her shirt up. Fallon hadn't dared to check while she was unconscious, but there they were: two long scars down her back, about two inches wide, more jagged and inflamed than Fallon's. Her eyes welled up with tears as she stared at them in the mirror. Victoria finally turned to her with a gaunt face and a quivering lip. "Fal?" she managed, her voice quiet from lack of use.

The tears fell down Fallon's cheeks as she reached out and pulled her close, pressing much harder than she should've. "Dove," she finally said.

Victoria huffed out a mix between a cry and a laugh before returning the embrace. Her hands gripped onto Fallon as her eyes closed tightly. "Is it really you?"

Fallon pulled back to look at her and grabbed her face. "Yes, it's me—what are you doing here? Did they—"

"No," she interrupted, shaking her head. "It's a long story...but I'll tell you that later." Victoria wrapped her arms around Fallon's waist and pressed her head against her chest. "I'm tired, and I missed you."

Fallon's mouth was open as she cried freely, astounded. When she finally moved, her hands went to Victoria's hair, where she held her still to make sure this was real. "Am I dreaming?"

"I hope not. It took a long time to find you," Victoria said against her skin.

When they pulled back, Fallon's eyes traced every line and crease on Victoria's face. "Tell me everything."

"The portal closed after I went through," Victoria told her with a lump in her throat. "I planned for him to come with me. I was going to pull him through so he could get out and figure the rest out from there, but..." She looked up at the ceiling to keep the tears from falling over. "When Dimitri and the archangels showed up, we weren't prepared. He fought them to give me time to escape." She picked at the remnants of a scab on her knee. "The last thing I saw was Dimitri standing over him while the archangels held him down." The tears finally fell, and she fell with them. Her hands cradled her head, snapping Fallon out of the image in her mind. She pulled Victoria into her side to keep her upright on the couch.

Victoria wiped her face with the back of her hand and sniffled. "I'm sorry, I don't know where that came from..."

Fallon dipped her head so they were eye level. "You should never apologize for having empathy, dove." She pushed aside a strand of hair and cupped the side of her face. "What you went through was traumatic; it'll take time to process everything you saw."

Victoria nodded, chewing on her lip. "How did you do it?" Her soft brown eyes were wide. "I'm practically a mess on the floor, and here *you* are," she waved her hand, "comforting *me.*"

Fallon sighed and rubbed her hand on Victoria's lower back in soothing circles. "Emil." When Victoria looked confused, she explained, "The man who owns the house we're in right now," with a chuckle. Victoria looked around as if she hadn't taken in her surroundings before that point. "He went into town a little while ago to get some fresh air. He's been cooped up in here with me since we found you."

"Why would he do that?" She wrapped her arms around herself. "He doesn't know me."

"No, but he knows me. I've been with him since I arrived here. It may be due to my own trauma, but we've gotten very close these past couple of months. He helped me figure out my life outside of Heaven."

Her eyes grew wide. "Does he—"

"No, he doesn't know. I haven't exactly figured out how to explain it to him, so I've avoided any questions by feigning either memory loss or sad memories. He's a kind man, and he's been very lenient and understanding with me."

Victoria offered a small smile. "I'm glad you had him." She sighed. "That doesn't make me feel any better about how you ended up here..." She eyed Fallon. "Speaking of which—", her smile disappeared. "We never spoke about how you ended up in that cell. Dimitri said you committed blasphemy, and...that's why you fell."

Fallon's face softened as she felt her walls slip away. She blinked slowly as she said, "I know."

"Is that—," Victoria stopped, and turned to face her on the couch. "Is it true?"

Fallon looked down at her hands on her lap. She knew her voice would crack, so she simply shrugged.

Victoria went deathly still on the couch, not blinking or breathing. When she could finally form words, they were quiet. "Why didn't you tell me?"

Fallon faced her. "Look at what happened when they found out." She threw her arm up at the sky in question. "The lengths they went to to get rid of me? To humiliate me? I didn't tell you because I wanted to avoid all of this." She let out a dry chuckle and dropped her shoulders. "Not that keeping quiet did me any good in the long run."

Victoria slowly looked around the room, collecting her thoughts. Then, her hand twitched toward Fallon. She retreated and then tried again. She placed her hand on top of Fallon's and picked up her arm. Fallon eyed her cautiously, too stunned to make a sound, while Victoria placed it around her shoulders. She leaned back until she was flush with the couch, Victoria leaning into her.

"What are you doing, dove?" Fallon whispered, terrified to disturb the peace.

After a moment of thought, she answered, "I don't know."

19

"I CAN'T BELIEVE YOU climbed through a window," Fallon mumbled through a mouth full of frikadeller.

Victoria laughed at her jumbled words as they strolled down the streets of Ribe. "It was my only option," she said, before taking her first bite. The moment the Danish meatballs met her tongue, she froze.

"What?" Fallon's mouth was full again.

"This is insane," she managed, which made Fallon choke on the bite in her mouth.

"Isn't it? Something about the food here is so much better than it was up there. The flavors are richer." Fallon licked the remnants off her fingers.

"It's not just—what do they call it, charcuterie all the time? I mean, how did we survive on snacks and pastries for so long?" She asked between bites.

Fallon shrugged. "The grass is always greener."

Victoria stopped chewing. "What does that mean?"

"It means that the other side of something always looks better. People want what they can't have, ya know?"

"Right..." She gave a short nod and kept walking, despite not knowing where they were headed. Fallon looped arms with her and pulled her down a side street, away from the cars and people.

"It's busier than normal today," she thought out loud.

"Probably because it's so beautiful outside," Victoria noted.

Arm in arm, Fallon watched her. "I'm really glad you're here."

Victoria smiled. "Me too, bun."

A close-lipped grin spread on Fallon's face when she decided to take Victoria to a stream nearby. Although they weren't in Heaven anymore, they could have a sense of normalcy. The walk was short and quiet, both of them finding solace in each other's company again. Fields of green stretched on both sides of the water, with marsh marigolds as a vibrant border between them and the stream.

Victoria sat down facing the water, crossing her legs beneath her. She stared out over the field with her hands in her lap, and words bouncing around in her head.

Fallon noticed the distance in her eyes. "Why did you come here, Vic?"

She turned her head, her eyes sad. "I told you, I missed you." Her voice was low, as if the marigolds might hear her.

Fallon knelt next to her. "I missed you too, don't get me wrong. But I made my decision; the seraphim warned me about what would happen if I didn't cooperate. I went willingly so you could live a normal life, and then..." She trailed off, leaving her thought unfinished.

"I couldn't let you be alone forever, Fal," she said before placing her hand on Fallon's thigh.

Fallon looked down at her touch. Her chest rose and fell without a word, and then she took Victoria's hand off her skin. "Don't...I can't—I left because—"

"I know why you left, Fallon." Victoria twisted on the grass so they faced each other. "Something Theo said made me look at myself, and I mean *really* look. When he sent me here, we didn't say a few special words and hope for the best, Lonnie. He told me I had to choose a memory; a memory that changed me forever, and it had to be about you."

Fallon fidgeted, feeling bare. "What did he say to you?"

A heavy sigh left Victoria while she debated repeating it. "He asked me how long I've been in love with you."

Fallon froze, her eyes trained on Victoria's face. She looked pale. "Please, Victoria...I can't have this conversation. I don't think I'm capable of hearing you say that you don't—"

"He was right." Her heart beat wildly in her chest while she prepared herself for the words she knew she had to say. "When he asked me to pick a memory that affected me? *Changed* me? I could barely pick one; there were too many. I realized that every decision I've made for decades has been with you in mind." She couldn't look her in the eyes. "I don't know when it started, and I don't know exactly what *it* is, but it scared me."

Fallon didn't look away. She didn't dare open her mouth, or cough, or blink.

"Am I making any sense? Do you know what I'm saying?"

An invitation.

With a breathy chuckle, Fallon told her, "I know exactly what you're saying." Victoria finally looked at her. Every thought she had in her cell ran through her mind in that moment, and she felt a wave of relief wash over her. "I know because...that's how it started for me," she confessed with a slight shrug.

Victoria bit her lip to keep from getting emotional. "Lonnie?"

Fallon couldn't help the well of tears that brimmed in her eyes. "Yeah, dove?"

She turned toward the water again and leaned into Fallon. "What do we do now?" she asked as the sun began to set.

Gingerly, like she could ruin the moment with a breath, she put her arm around Victoria's shoulders. "I'm not sure." Victoria sighed, letting her weight rest against Fallon, who shut her eyes tight, not sure what to do with herself. Finally, she said, "I think, now, we live."

Victoria turned her head upward to look at Fallon.

"We owe that to ourselves, right?" Fallon asked as she looked at the sunset. "We did everything right. We kept our heads down, and we did our jobs well. They locked me in a room and threatened me until I finally cracked—," her voice broke, and she sniffled. "They ripped off my wings—a treasured piece of me—and threw me away like I was garbage."

Victoria watched as a tear fell down her cheek. She let it fall.

"It took me too long to learn, but I deserve to be happy." She looked down at Victoria's upturned face. "And so do you." Her hand rested on Victoria's cheek. "And then you did the same to yourself." A laugh broke out of her. "They made you feel so unsafe, so unwanted, that you found a way out." Fallon started rocking to self-soothe. "I thought I was okay without you. I didn't go to bed crying anymore, I could see something in your favorite color and not feel like my feet were kicked out from under me. Things were looking up, it seemed." She shook her head, mouth agape. "And then I saw you. And I realized that none of that had gone away. I had just accepted that there was no hope I would ever see you again... It seemed like I had no other choice but to keep going."

"And now?" Victoria finally broke her silence.

When Fallon looked back down at her, her muscles eased. Her chest felt lighter. "Now," she rubbed Victoria's arm, "I realize how much I discredited you. You did all this...for me?"

Victoria nodded slowly. Telling Theo was one thing; looking at the reason for her break in character was an entirely different story.

"You amaze me."

Victoria sat up, making Fallon's arm fall. She didn't want her moving away to undo her confession, so she stopped her. "Don't move."

Fallon flinched and swatted around her face. "Why, is there a bug?"

"No, gosh, don't move!"

Fallon went deathly still.

"Close your eyes."

Fallon did as she said.

She felt strong; taking control of the situation made it a bit easier—like she had power. She *never* felt that in Heaven. After a beat, Victoria slowly leaned forward with her eyes open. She watched Fallon's face as she inched closer and closer until, finally, their lips brushed.

Fallon's breath hitched, and her lashes threatened to flutter open. "I said don't move," Victoria reminded her, and she turned to stone again.

With open eyes, Victoria took a deep breath in. The movement brought her lips to touch Fallon's, but she moved no further. She sat there, perfectly still, watching Fallon's shaky breaths. She inclined her head, their noses brushing. Something about the skin contact brought her a sense of peace, despite her heart racing in her chest. After a moment, she leaned back. Fallon opened her eyes, slowly. The look on her face was almost giddy, and Victoria smiled softly at her. "I don't know what I'm doing," she confessed.

Fallon threw her head back and stared at the sky. "Neither do I." She turned to look at Victoria's hand, and put hers over it, delicately, like her fingers might shatter against the grass. Victoria watched as Fallon's hand rested on hers, her thumb swiping back and forth against her skin. Neither of them moved, watching a sunset they had no part in creating.

"What do you think they're doing without us?" Victoria asked into the dimness.

Fallon chuckled dryly. "Look at the sky, Vic. They're scrambling up there."

20

"WHAT DO YOU GIRLS want for dinner?" Emil asked from the barn.

Fallon knelt on the ground next to the small garden to help Victoria place markers in the soil. "Anything but pork belly. I feel sluggish."

Victoria's hands were covered in soil, dirt caked beneath her nails. "Oooh, what about fish?"

Emil made a delighted sound and clapped the animal dander off his hands. "I like where your head is. I think the market I get my cod at is closed by now," he said while stroking his facial hair.

"Weren't you telling us just the other day that you're an incredible fisherman? I bet you could catch some yourself," Fallon said while piling soil onto a newly placed marker.

He adjusted the waist of his pants as he thought. "I bet I could." Emil looked at the two of them, busy tending to their garden, and decided to go alone. "I shouldn't be gone too long. Stay out of trouble, and Fallon, don't forget to feed—"

"I know, I know. Shirl wouldn't let me forget to feed her."

He walked over and put his semi-dirty hand on the top of her head and shook it playfully. "Always 'I know', with you. You don't know everything, kid."

She looked at him with playful eyes. "That's what *you* think."

Emil pushed her head before walking back into the barn to grab a fishing pole. "When you're finished naming those plants, could you start a fire?"

Victoria giggled. "Naming the vegetables," she said under her breath. "We will!" she called out to him.

Fallon waved to him as he pulled away from the house and started down the road. The second she turned around, Victoria was behind her. "Finished already?"

She nodded and pointed at the carrots. "This one's name is Angela." Fallon raised a brow at her, amused, and Victoria laughed again. Before they went inside, they made sure the animals had everything they needed before turning in for the night. When the last chicken was accounted for, Victoria held out her hand. "I have something I want to show you."

Intrigued, Fallon latched their hands together and followed her back to the house, into what had become their shared bedroom. Victoria patted the bed, guiding Fallon to sit. She then went to a small dresser on the opposite wall and pulled out a roll of silky blue ribbon.

"Where'd you get that?" They'd spent almost every minute together since she arrived.

"I asked Emil to grab it for me when we split up the other day. I told him I needed ribbon for my hair."

"Did you?"

Victoria shook her head. "I wanted to try something." She began to unspool the ribbon. "The other day? When I, um..." Her eyes looked hopeful.

"What about it, dove?"

"It felt good. Taking things at my own pace, being in control..." She started to curl in on herself, but Fallon insisted she keep going. "I started to wonder what other ways I could feel like that. And, well, I got to thinking..."

Her uncharacteristic timidness made Fallon smile. "What *are* you thinking?"

Victoria bit her lip. "I'd like to try that again—getting close to you."

Fallon's stomach dropped. "Alright," she said with curious eyes. "What's the ribbon for?"

"Do you trust me?" Fallon nodded, and Victoria motioned for her to hold out her hands. She wrapped a section of the ribbon around her wrists three times. Not tight enough to be painful, she could get out of it if she tried. "Is this okay?" Fallon nodded, silent, watching as Victoria cut the strand from the spool and tied it in a neat bow.

The dim light of the candles flickered against the soft blue ribbon. Fallon turned her arms over, watching the light hit the bindings on her arms. She inspected them, knowing Victoria watched her carefully.

"Does it hurt?"

Fallon shook her head. "No, not it all. It feels soft," she tried to pull her arms apart, "but firm."

Victoria smiled. "Good."

"This will help you feel better about touching me?"

Victoria shrugged. "I'm not entirely sure. I figured it was worth a shot, though." She picked up Fallon's arms and traced the edges of the ribbon with her fingertip. "I had a lot of time to think while we were apart," she said as her eyes flicked up to meet Fallon's. "I don't think I'm ready to meet you where you are." She wrapped her fingers around Fallon's wrists. "But I know I would like to. This," she wiggled her tied arms, "seems like a way for me to maintain some control. *If* it's something you're comfortable with..." Fallon smiled at her. "What?"

"I just can't believe this is happening." Her voice was soft and breathy. "I denied my feelings for—well, a long time, until they finally bubbled up and I couldn't keep them down. I love our friendship more than anything. I never wanted to make you feel uncomfortable or scared or—or risk the chance of you not feeling the way I did. And now," she held up her wrists in between their faces, making them both laugh. "Whatever methods you want to try to understand yourself, I'm in. I know it isn't fair of me to ask you to be as ready as I am. I'd be happy just to have you in my life, dove."

Victoria picked up her hands and placed a small kiss on both of her thumbs. "Thank you," she mumbled against her knuckles.

"I kind of like it," she said with a shimmy.

Victoria pushed her shoulder playfully. "Good. I think I'd cave in on myself if I made you uncomfortable."

Fallon lifted her still-bound hands with sultry eyes. "Now, untie me so I can hold you."

Face flushed, she listened. She watched her own hands unravel the soft blue ribbon, while Fallon watched her face. Hands free, Fallon pulled back the sheets and slowly leaned back, bringing Victoria with her, until their bodies were flush under the covers. Neither of them spoke, their chests rising and falling in tandem. Fallon couldn't help but trace circles on Victoria's skin, amused by the goosebumps that followed where she went.

"I'm due for a manicure."

Victoria's head slowly shifted, groggy from having fallen asleep. "I came all this way for you to use me for a manicure?"

Fallon chuckled into Victoria's hair before breathing in her dark, coarse waves. "I missed you, dove." She couldn't see her face, but she heard the smile in her voice.

"I missed you, too, bun."

She hadn't meant to fall asleep, but Fallon startled when a door closed in the house.

"Girls?" Emil called out into the quiet house.

She looked down at Victoria's peaceful face and couldn't bear the idea of waking her, so she slithered from behind her and crept out of the room. When Emil didn't see Victoria with her, he asked if she was alright.

"She's okay, she just fell asleep. I think she's still adjusting to everything."

"Speaking of which..." he trailed. Fallon had become so comfortable with Emil, that it no longer occurred to her that he didn't know the full extent of their past. "I try not to ask about things that aren't my business." He put his hands up, defensive. "You both clearly went through a lot before you ended up here, and I respect your privacy. But I need to know, Fallon." He closed the space between them and put a hand on the outside of her arm. "Was someone hurting you back home?"

Fallon's face twisted at the memory of Dimitri's grip on her wings, but she shook her head. "It's not like that...it's really complicated."

Emil nodded slowly with pursed lips and took a seat in one of the wooden dining chairs. He propped an ankle on his thigh and stared at her. "I've got time."

With a sigh, Fallon leaned against the kitchen counter and told him *everything*.

After an hour of uninterrupted rambling, Fallon crossed her arms and stared at Emil, whose mouth had fallen open one minute in, and hadn't closed.

"So—you were both...angels." He put his hands on each of his thighs. "Living in the clouds, in Heaven, until they..." His head shot up. "Until they took your wings?"

Fallon nodded, close-lipped.

"All because you two are in love with each other?"

She exhaled through her nose. "They went after me first. I apparently wasn't very good at keeping my feelings private. Anyone who looked at us knew how I felt about her, and *she*, well...I don't think she knew until recently."

Emil stared at the ceiling with his hand cupped against his jaw, repeatedly tousling the hair on his chin while nodding to himself. After what felt like an eternity to Fallon, he stood from the dining chair and approached her slowly. Fallon's lip started to quiver before her face connected with his chest, and he enveloped her in his arms. She didn't cry, although she wanted to. It felt like she *should*. Tremors racked her body while Emil soothingly petted her hair, mumbling more to himself than to her.

"It's so unfair," he said.

Fallon could only nod.

He didn't try to pull away or leave the room, even after they sat there for four minutes. Emil didn't shift his feet until Fallon felt strong enough to stand on her own. When he could see her face, he held it. "You're not broken, Fallon."

Her lip began to tremble again, this time with the threat of tears. "Are you sure?"

Emil's chest ached at her question, having wondered the same about himself when he was younger. "Who you love, and how you love them—that's personal. That's *yours*." He pointed at her chest. "No one—no man, angel, or any god can take that from you."

Fallon watched as a stream of tears fell down his cheeks, and she hurt for him; she knew he was speaking to both of them. "Then why am I down here?" she whispered with a shrug. "I had everything I ever wanted; I wished for nothing. I loved my job, my home—my wings?" Her head fell back as she closed her eyes. "What if I don't know who I am without Heaven?"

"You're Fallon. You're smart, and you're funny." He sniffled. "You're great with animals, and you're a mean cook." The corner of her mouth lifted, despite her look of disbelief, and he continued. "You're creative and passionate about the things you love. And one of those," he pointed toward the hallway, "is here now. She followed you from the Heavens, Fallon." He cradled her hands in his calloused ones. "Can you really say you had everything you wanted?"

Fallon turned her head toward their room and slowly shook her head in realization. "No. I didn't." She wiped her nose with the back of her hand before looking at the ground. "They locked me in a cell," she said sternly. When she looked at him again, her eyes were angry. "They kept me from her and interrogated me. All for what?" Her hands went into her hair, gripping at the roots. "They preach love and acceptance and forgiveness," she began pacing, "unless you step out of the perfect white box. Then they sweep you into the shadows and try to convince you that you're wrong for feeling that way." Fallon balled her fists and pushed them against her eyes. "They ripped off my *wings*," she seethed. When she moved her hands, Emil was nodding.

"They didn't deserve you—either of you." He pulled her into him again and felt the tension in her body ease. "You have a home here, you know."

She craned her neck to look at him. "What?"

He shrugged. "I don't have any other family, kid. When my mom passed, August got me through it. And now that August is gone too..." He sighed. "It's just me around here. I've got a lot of farm, and only two legs. You're already set up in that room; it's yours."

Fallon's arms wrapped around him with a squeeze. Her fists clenched, holding him tight. "Thanks," she said before sniffling. "I don't think I would've been okay if you hadn't found me."

"Let's not think about that," he told her as he patted her head. "Eat a snack for me, would you, søde? Then you can go back to bed."

After scarfing down leftovers, she craned her head to look at him. "I've been meaning to ask, what does that mean anyway?"

"Sweetie." He approached her at the kitchen sink while she rinsed her plate, and tousled her hair with his calloused hands. "Now get some rest, kid."

21

V ICTORIA FLINCHED AWAY FROM the wriggling
worm between Emil's fingers.

"I'm not touching that," she said sternly.

"How are you gonna put it on the hook without touching
it?" Fallon stood next to her and cast her line into the water.
"It's definitely a little gross, but you get used to it." She leaned
closer and whispered, "And if nothing bites, you don't have
to put on more bait."

Victoria squinted at her. "How are you so good at this?"

Fallon giggled. "I am *not.* Emil took me out here to clear my head. He taught me how to hook the bait, how to cast; I wasn't allowed to go home until I caught something." Victoria's eyebrows rose. "We were out here for a while..." She held the pole between her knees and held out her hand for the worm. She shivered when it first landed in her hand, but quickly recovered so Victoria wouldn't see. With a pinch, she put the worm on Victoria's hook and wiped her hands before picking up her own pole. "See? Not so bad."

Mouth agape, Victoria watched her smear dirt and worm residue on her jeans.

"Since when are you scared of dirt and bugs? You're the gardener here, not me!" Fallon reminded her with a smirk.

"Oh, I'm sorry; I don't usually pick up the bugs and jab them with things while I'm planting cucumbers," she said before attempting to cast. "It's inhumane," she decided as she dropped her shoulders with her unmoving pole.

"It's the circle of life," Fallon told her. She didn't miss how Emil chuckled under his breath at her using his exact response from *her* first time. Before she could say anything else, something pulled on her line. She quickly started reeling, her heart racing from excitement, until she reminded herself to loosen the line a bit.

"What are you doing? It's going to get away!" Victoria shouted.

"I thought it was *inhumane*," she said with a smirk. "Besides, if you pull your hardest, the line will break. You can only pull for so long before it snaps." She began reeling it toward her again.

"Can't it just eat the worm and get away if you do that? Isn't the whole point to catch one?" Her brows were furrowed, her forehead creased with concern.

Fallon watched her instead of the fish she was fighting. She smiled, finding it silly. "Everything happens for a reason, right? If I don't catch this fish, it wasn't the fish for me. Maybe it was sick or had a fish family or something. What's meant for me will find me. Aren't we proof of that?" Before Victoria could respond, the fish broke through the water, its silvery skin a rainbow of colors. "See?" she asked, matter-of-factly.

Emil stood by, ready to take the fish off her hook. "Nice one, søde! We can cook this one, or we can pickle it. I'll leave it up to you since it's your catch."

Fallon's proud smile was all Victoria could look at, having completely forgotten about her own baited hook floating in the water. She watched as the hook popped from the fish's mouth, and Emil put it into the cooler he brought with them. She didn't realize her face had twisted.

"If it bothers you that much, dove, you don't have to keep fishing. We can use the bait already on your hook, so it doesn't go to waste, and we can head home. Does that sound okay?"

Victoria looked at this new woman. Usually, it was *her* comforting *Fallon,* not the other way around. She hadn't realized how anxious she had become without her. Emil caught another herring, one a bit larger, and began packing up their things. When he stepped away, Victoria grabbed Fallon's arm. "You seem different here. More...confident."

Fallon shrugged, but she had noticed it too. "I think—," she tried to find the words. "I think I was always so focused on what others were thinking of me, if they were looking at me. I was constantly worried that one of them would see the way I looked at you and report me to an archangel. Despite everything that happened, I'm... I feel good."

It made Victoria jealous. It had been two weeks since she fell to Earth, and the bad dreams hadn't stopped. It was always the same moment; Theo's face smushed against the ground while she reached for the portal. She didn't feel good; she felt tired. She felt scared, like at any moment a seraph would show up and drag her away from the life she was just starting. Seraphim be damned, she would plant her fingers in the ground until her nails bled as they dragged her away. She felt Fallon's hand on her arm, and she flinched.

"You ready to go home?" Her face was concerned, but she knew it wasn't the time or place. She knew she had looked the same at some point.

Victoria nodded. "Yeah. Let's go," she said quietly.

Fallon watched her stare out the window as the trees passed in a blur of green and brown the entire way home. They decided to pickle the herring so Victoria could try something new, although it wouldn't be ready for about a week. Fallon whipped up a chicken salad with mushrooms Victoria picked from the garden, while Emil cooked some bacon. He chopped and sprinkled it onto their team effort meal before running off to tend to the animals one last time before he turned in for the night.

"Do you want to talk about what happened at the lake?"

Victoria figured it was coming, but hadn't prepared what she would say. "You're so free here, Fal. Why don't I feel that way?"

Fallon knew exactly what she meant. "This feeling doesn't happen overnight. In fact, I *still* have days where I'm not sure if any of this is real—like I'm going to wake up tomorrow in that cell."

"Fal..." she sighed, and placed a comforting hand on her wrist.

"I know. But then I wake up, and I'm not in the cell. I'm in a comfortable bed in the home of someone who cared enough to take me in. I wake up next to my best friend, who fought tooth and nail to get to me. And I promise you, Victoria," she flipped her hand and latched their fingers, "that it will get better. It may take longer than you hope it will, or it could happen before you expect it. One day, you could open your eyes and think, 'I can't believe I went through that.' There's no way of knowing. But here? We have a chance, dove; a *real* chance to live without fear of persecution."

Victoria nodded slowly, letting the words fall over her like rain. "I hope we get that."

"I do too, Vic." She rubbed her thumb against the top of Victoria's hand. "Why don't we clean up dinner and get ready for bed, huh? Wash off the outside, and get cozy."

That made her smile. "I'd like that."

Victoria showered first, taking her time. Steam built up on the mirror while her muscles eased under the scalding water. She had finally gotten the remnants of the day off her skin and reached for her towel—her fingers closing around damp air where her towel should be. "Fallon?" she called out from inside the shower.

After a few moments, Fallon put her face near the door. "Are you alright?" she asked from the hall.

"I think I forgot my towel on the foot of the bed. Could you grab it for me?" When she didn't hear a response, she stepped out of the shower to see if she could find one in the cabinet beside the sink. She had just grabbed the handle when the door opened, revealing Fallon, towel in hand. Her first instinct was to cover herself, awkwardly positioning her arms to conceal her chest.

"Shoot, Vic, I'm sorry! I thought you'd still be in the shower," Fallon rushed out before closing the door.

Victoria stood naked in the bathroom with her lips pulled into her mouth and her eyes closed. "It's alright," she croaked. Her cheeks were as bright as cherries. They'd changed in front of each other before, sure, but one of them always turned their back. She took a calming breath to right herself—she thought she might die if her voice cracked. "Thank you," she said, and then stuck her arm into the hall with an open hand. Fallon placed the towel in her grasp and scurried back to their bedroom, fanning her face.

That wasn't how Fallon had imagined it happening. She always hoped it would be by candlelight after an afternoon of painting and baking—not by mistake, followed by both of them shutting down. She was sitting on the edge of the bed, biting her nails, when Victoria came into the room with the towel wrapped around her. She knew Victoria was embarrassed, even though she didn't do anything wrong.

"I thought when you didn't answer, it meant you hadn't heard me," Victoria explained while pulling on her night clothes.

"No, no, I get it. That makes sense, looking at it now. I should have said something; that's my mistake," Fallon answered while staring at the wall. When she turned, Victoria's bottom lip was between her teeth. She stared directly at it. "What if we tried something different tonight?"

Victoria's brows rose as she quirked her head. "What did you have in mind?"

Before she could consider if it would work or not, Fallon reached into the nightstand and pulled out the wad of ribbon. "I think tonight," she held it out between them, "it's your turn."

"My turn?" Victoria's neck craned forward, the crease in her forehead prominent.

"If you're willing to try, of course. I'm wondering if it being *out* of your control will feel better than having to make the decisions yourself." She positioned her own hands in the same way Victoria had done to her, and waited for an answer. Just as she began to think it was a mistake, Victoria held out her hands.

"I'm intrigued. Nervous, but..."

"Curious?" Fallon asked with a quirked brow. Victoria nodded sheepishly and mirrored Fallon's hand placement. Fallon made quick work of wrapping the ribbon around her wrists and tied it off with a small bow. "Can I try something else?" Victoria nodded again, but Fallon squinted. "I need you to tell me, dove. If we're going to do this, we have to be transparent. I need to hear your voice to know you're here with me."

"I'm okay," she assured her. "I want to try."

Fallon put her finger under Victoria's chin and tilted her head. "I'm not going to wrap it tight. If you want me to stop, you tell me." Fallon knelt before Victoria's legs, which dangled off the side of the bed, and slowly wound the ribbon around her calves. She continued, bringing it up to her knees, and checked on her again. "Does this feel okay?"

"It's not tight," Victoria whispered, her voice breathy.

"Good." Fallon smiled up at her from the floor and wrapped the strand of ribbon around Victoria's knees. "Can you kneel on the bed?"

"I'm actually not sure," she laughed. She swung her bound legs over the edge and fell sideways onto the bed. With the side of her face against the covers, her breath came out short, and her heart raced.

Fallon noticed the change in attention, so she stopped. "Here, let me help." She slid her hands between Victoria's side and the bed, lifting her to a kneeling position. "Is that better?"

"Yes, sorry... I didn't like that feeling."

Fallon's hands froze. "You have nothing to apologize for." She pushed Victoria's hair behind her ear and placed a kiss on her forehead. "Why don't we stop there? This seems like enough adventure for one night, I think." She moved to unwrap Victoria's legs, but she shook her head.

"No, please! I feel better now, I'm alright. Keep going." Her brows were dipped, pleading.

Fallon stared directly into Victoria's eyes and froze, contemplating. She decided to ride the strange high they were both on, and keep going while they felt up to it. She passed the ribbon to herself behind Victoria's body, her fingers brushing the front and back of her thighs each time. She saw the goosebumps that appeared, and she smirked. They both knew the feeling, now. Fallon tried not to think about how close they were. She also tried not to think about the fact that Victoria's chest was right next to her face as she worked to bind her legs.

Or the way it felt to kneel before her.

She tried not to think about it.

Out of ribbon and skin buzzing, she stood from the bed and looked at Victoria. "How do you feel, dove?"

Victoria looked down at herself and examined the silky blue against her skin. Fallon followed her line of sight and noticed how the freckles and beauty marks on her legs were framed by the crossing of the ribbon. By the time she looked back at her face, Victoria was already watching her.

"It feels...different." She shifted, her skin pushing against her constraints. "Good different."

Fallon didn't miss how she fidgeted. "That's good," she managed to say before clearing her throat. She leaned forward, clenched her jaw, and began unraveling Victoria. It took the entirety of her iron will not to turn her head. She was so close to Victoria's face that she could smell the shampoo they both used—lavender scented. With the bundle of ribbon in her hands, she began to pull away.

"Fallon." Victoria's voice was barely above a whisper.

She froze. "Yes, dove?" Fallon failed to resist temptation and quirked her head to gaze into the eyes that felt like home. When they flicked down, her breath hitched. A shivering breath filled the space between them before Victoria leaned in, and her eyes fluttered shut.

Victoria wasn't going to let fear dictate the rest of their lives. She made it out, and she intended to use her time wisely; to really *live*.

With that thought in the back of her mind, she made her decision. Her heartbeat was irregular, almost erratic, as she tilted her face and pressed her lips to Fallon's, who welcomed the touch. Their mouths collided like clouds brushing against one another in the sky. With her hands free from the ribbon, Victoria reached for Fallon's skin. Her arm, her shoulder, her leg—anything she could feel against her chilled fingers.

Fallon's hand cupped Victoria's face as her lips lingered, desperately wishing time would freeze in that moment. It didn't, and Victoria pulled away as Fallon was preparing to deepen their kiss. She dipped her head down, pressing her forehead against Fallon's.

"Wow," she breathed.

The smile plastered to Fallon's face couldn't waver as she echoed, "Yeah, wow," and placed her hand on the back of Victoria's neck. They sat on the bed, silently sharing breath. Once she was able to collect her thoughts, she pulled Victoria into her side and leaned back against the headboard. "That was...unexpected."

Victoria let out a breathy chuckle. "I just—"

She didn't finish the thought, so Fallon encouraged her. "What's going on in your pretty head, hm?"

The compliment made Victoria blush, no matter how many times she heard it. "I wanted to, so I did." She craned her neck and looked at Fallon. "Is that crazy?"

Fallon shook her head and pulled her in closer by her shoulder. "You're asking the woman they threw from Heaven for being in love with you." Immediately after she said it, she gasped. Any confidence she had built was swept out from under her by her own words. "I—um..."

But Victoria knew. Even if it scared her, she knew. "Shh, shh." She wiggled to reposition herself against Fallon. "I know, bun. I know."

22

V ICTORIA WAITED UNTIL FALLON was sleeping heavily before slinking away to the bathroom. She splashed some cold water on her face and braced her arms on the sink.

Theo's words still bounced in her head, shouting louder than anything else. *How long have you been in love with her?* She still didn't have an answer. Every time she thought about it, her hands turned clammy.

Victoria repeatedly reminded herself that she was safe, that no one was coming to get them. In reality, their homes in the clouds likely had new owners. Their aprons and lockers were probably occupied by another willing body. In the end, that was all they were.

Bodies.

She was happy to be alive and well, something she couldn't say with certainty about Theo. She thought about him every day, how unfair it was that she made it out and he had been captured. Theo was the reason she knew about the memory bridge. Without him, she would never have seen Fallon again. Held her again. Kissed her—well, ever.

She *kissed* her.

The thought made her heart flutter, but it also made her feel guilty. She hadn't realized it before, but she couldn't dive into her future without knowing what happened to Theo. If she were to accept her feelings for Fallon, it would be with a clean conscience. How she planned on doing that, she had no idea. But it could wait until morning. She would sleep with her thoughts, and hope that all her questions would be answered in her dreams.

Hopeful? Perhaps, but Victoria had made it this far. Far from her garden, her things, her home, her friends. They all paled in comparison to the woman waiting with open arms just in the other room. She would be present, *and* she would find answers. Even if it meant leaving her comfort zone once again.

Having found some solace in the cool water on her face, she returned to their shared room and crawled back into bed beside Fallon. An hour passed before she was able to fall asleep, finding it all too easy to watch Fallon's still face in the darkness. She didn't have to speak or know the answers to the questions in her head. She could lie there with her feelings until the sun rose, if she wished, and no one would bother her.

When she woke that next morning, it was like she hadn't slept at all. She opened her eyes to find Fallon's arm resting on her waist, her hand tucked under her side; a human seatbelt latching her to the bed. If she stayed still, the moment wouldn't end—she could soak in the contact a while longer.

Fallon was already awake, doing the exact same thing. "Hey, sleepy head," she mumbled.

Victoria sighed lightly through her nose. "Good morning," she replied as she turned under Fallon's hold, making them face-to-face.

"Did you sleep okay?"

Victoria thought about lying. After a moment of reflection, she decided it was best to be honest if she wanted a future built on trust with Fallon. It was the first time she had considered that: a future with Fallon. "No, actually. I didn't." Fallon's brow furrowed, calling to Victoria's fingers to smooth it out again. "I've been thinking about Theo." She chewed on the inside of her cheek, needing somewhere to put her restless energy.

"Oh, dove, I'm sorry." She pulled the arm around her waist and brought her close. "I can't imagine the weight you must feel."

Tucked against her chest, she felt safe enough to share. "He risked everything for me. He threw away his own chance at happiness so I could have a fresh start and...I don't even know where he is."

"Maybe they made him stay in Heaven. No longer as a prize, but as punishment for finding a loophole."

It hurt to hear, but Fallon made sense. "I think you're right. I just wish there was a way I could show him that I'm alright, you know? That I found you, and we're okay." She turned her head into Fallon's neck and rested there as she fought back tears.

Fallon shifted to a sitting position with Victoria still tucked against her. "Maybe we can—," she thought out loud. Victoria looked at her, and she hesitated. "This may sound silly, but what if..." She trailed off.

"What if *what*, Fal?"

She smirked. "What if we sent a message the same way you came?"

Victoria's shoulders dropped, disappointed. "That won't work. Once you've crossed the pons memoriae, you can't go back. You only get one chance, and I've used mine," she recalled from the book.

Fallon sighed, thinking. She quirked her head, and Victoria waited for what she knew was another idea brewing in her head. "What if we sent something else through? A symbol, something he would recognize. You open the gate with a memory, but does it have to be a person who goes through?"

Victoria sat up straight. "I...I don't know. It wasn't a question I needed to answer at the time, I didn't think to ask." She looked at Fallon, intrigued. "What did you have in mind?"

Fallon smiled and ripped away the covers. "Let's go."

Victoria followed her through the halls with a giddy, yet curious smile. Fallon's steps were sure as they walked through the kitchen, where Emil sat at the table, still groggy from sleep.

"There you both are," he said, closing the morning paper. He cocked a brow at their expectant faces. "Where are you off to?"

Fallon's smile showed her teeth; she was so excited. "Off to run an errand. Be back soon!"

"When?" he asked over the rim of his coffee mug.

"Soon!" she cheered, reaching for the doorknob.

Emil chuckled at her intensity. She closed the door behind them and began running toward the back of the barn.

"Where are we going?" Victoria shouted from behind.

Fallon stopped running and grabbed Victoria's hands. "To your piece of mind, I hope."

In hopeful silence, Victoria followed her through the field, past a copse of trees and into the clearing surrounded by flowers. "What is this place?" she finally asked.

Fallon stopped in the middle of the field and turned to her. "The first few days after I woke up, I felt so *lost*. This place was unfamiliar to me, and I was still reeling from the fact that I had lost you forever." Victoria took a step toward her. "In my grief, I walked. Away from the farm, away from the house, from the noise. I needed quiet to wallow freely. So, I came here," she waved her arms toward the brightly colored trees and flowers. "When I did, I made an unexpected friend—one that stunned me into a revelation: everything would be okay. I didn't know how, or when, but I knew I would get through it all." She held out her hand, and a single white dove flew from the tallest tree and landed on her fingers like a perch.

"Is that..." Victoria took a careful step forward, not wanting to startle the creature.

Fallon nodded with a proud smile. "Dove, meet *dove*." She stretched her arm out toward Victoria, the bright white bird on her hand chirping lightly as she quirked her head to investigate.

"She's beautiful." She reached toward the bird and slowly extended her hand to touch her. The bird inclined her head before leaning into Victoria's hand.

"When I saw her, a wave of calm came over me. I took her as a sign that I would recover and heal." She looked at Victoria, who now held the bird close to her face, fawning over her. "I had no idea how right that would be. It never occurred to me that I would see you again, let alone be near you again, outside of my dreams."

Victoria smiled, but she was still a little confused. "How is she going to help me talk to Theo?"

Fallon positioned her hand so the bird could step back onto it. "She's going to take a little trip," she explained while stroking her feathers with a single finger. "We can use some of our ribbon to attach a note to her leg, and have her fly through. We could lead her right to Theo, and hopefully ease your mind." She switched from petting the bird to Victoria, placing her hand at the back of her neck. "You deserve to be happy."

Victoria watched the dove look between the two of them and wondered if she knew what they were saying. "Could you do that for us?" The bird chittered, which further convinced her they were on the same page. After a moment of contemplation, she looked at Fallon.

"Do you remember the words Theo said to get the portal to open?" It was the only piece Fallon didn't have.

She chewed on her lip and thought hard. "I think I remember most of it. I would need to practice, but I'm sure I could figure it out. That day sort of plays over and over in my mind."

Fallon lifted her hand toward the sky, and the bird took flight. "Whenever you're ready, Victoria. There's no rush. I just wanted you to know that there's always hope."

23

"**I** THINK I GOT it!"

Fallon's head snapped up from the dough in front of her. "Really?!" It had been three days since Fallon took Victoria into the grove. With flour up to her elbows, she wiped her arms on the apron Emil got for her and walked to the table, where Victoria had pages of notes scattered all over it.

"I had been stuck on one part in the middle. I was so sure of the wording, but every time I tried, nothing would open.

I had to step away from it for a while, and then something clicked in my head." She snapped her notebook shut and looked at Fallon's project on the counter. "Let that rise, Fal. We have a portal to open."

While Fallon hurriedly scrubbed the baking mess from her arms, Victoria tore a strip of paper from her notebook. She had thought about what she would say if she had the chance for a while now. But when she put pencil to paper, nothing happened. Her head was so fogged with what would happen next that she couldn't focus.

Fallon noticed her hesitance as she dried her hands with a small brown rag, and stood over her. "Nervous?"

Victoria huffed out a laugh. "I don't know why. This is what I've wanted, and now I have a real chance to do it. Why do I feel so stuck?" She rested her head in her hands and sighed.

Fallon had felt the same way—the feeling almost disabled her when Victoria first arrived at the farm. She knelt next to her and grabbed her hands, cradling them in her own. "Look at me, Vic." She heard a sniffle and reached for Victoria's face beneath her cascading brown hair. When her scared eyes met Fallon's understanding ones, her breathing slowed.

"What if this doesn't work? What if Theo never knows what happened to me, and he's stuck in Heaven, unhappy, forever?" Her hands left a mark where they pressed to her forehead, making her troubled face a brighter shade of pink.

"You can spend your entire life wondering 'what if'. What if I didn't lose my wings? What if I had never spoken to Dimitri that day? What if..." Her throat bobbed. "What if we never met?" The pain in Victoria's eyes at the thought of it settled something in Fallon. "My point is, you'll never know if you don't try. It may not work, you're right. But what if it *does*? Imagine the look on Theo's face when he sees that all of his time, all of his effort, *meant* something. Don't you think that's worth the chance?"

Victoria chewed on her lip while her fingers twisted into a strand of her hair. "Let's do it," she finally decided.

Fallon reached out a hand toward Victoria. "You've got this." Fingers intertwined, they walked past the barn to the grove where their small, feathered friend sat on a low-hanging branch. It watched as they strolled through the field with purpose, buzzing with nerves. When Fallon held out the hand not attached to Victoria, the bird flew to it without pause. "Hi, little one. Are you ready to do something for us?" The bird leapt into the air, wings spread. It circled them twice, chirping a happy song as it spun. Fallon smiled at Victoria. "I think she knows."

With shaking hands, Victoria opened her notebook and placed it on the ground in front of them. She looked between

Fallon and the dove, which was back on Fallon's hand. She reached down and tore the note she wrote to Theo out of the book before swiping a finger over it. She had scribbled out and restarted the letter a handful of times, trying to write something that conveyed the weight of her gratitude. After several empty-feeling letters, she stopped filtering her thoughts and decided to get straight to the point.

"Theo,

You saved my life.

I hadn't allowed myself to think too much about my future; there was no reason to question it. I knew that I would wake up, paint my dreams into the sky, and life would go on. Running into you in the archives changed the trajectory of my being.

I found Fallon. We're safe, I'm happy, and I have you to thank.

I never got to answer your question; I was too scared to acknowledge my answer:

Forever."

She looked up at Fallon, who was stroking the bird's wings longingly, and folded the note tight. She poked her nail through the corner and managed to fit the ribbon through the opening before approaching her messenger. "May I?" The bird cooed, calling Victoria to step closer and secure the ribbon to her leg. She tied it carefully and stroked the bird's head softly when she finished. She knelt on the warm grass before her notebook and took a steadying breath.

Fallon mimicked what Victoria always told her when she was anxious. "What can you see, Vic?"

Victoria smiled softly. "Flowers." She turned to her right. "An oak tree." When she turned to her left, Fallon was eyeing her with a gentle expression, the corner of her mouth quirked to the side, proud. "I see you," she finished. With a clear head, she began reciting the spell—quietly at first, her volume rising as her nerves waned.

"Haec memoria ad me locum perveniat, quem videre non possum..." She opened her hands, her palms toward the sky, soaking in the last few drops of late afternoon sunlight. "Satis sit, sint omnia. Utere hac fenestra in animam meam, et recipe me in cor meum."

The memory she chose to open the portal was a newer one. It was the moment she realized where her urgency came from; why the idea of being without Fallon made her hands clammy and her heart race.

She closed her eyes and played the conversation in her head—the night it finally clicked.

Victoria was in love with Fallon.

As she neared the end of the memory, she felt a small gust of wind, and the corners of her mouth lifted. It was *working*.

The portal swooshed as her thoughts came to a close. She opened her eyes to meet Fallon's, who was already grinning ear to ear in awe of the intensity on Victoria's face. Fallon moved her hand closer to the whirling purple cloud as the dove adjusted its feet for flight. Victoria stood and thanked the dove earnestly—for some reason, she was certain the bird understood her.

The moment the words left her mouth, the dove flew through the portal. Both Fallon and Victoria watched intently, waiting to see if the bird would be denied passage by the spell. After a moment, the whirling slowed, and the cloud faded into nothing.

They hadn't realized it with the commotion from the portal, but the grove had turned completely silent. No air rustled the trees; the usual bird sounds and distant noise from moving water had ceased. With the portal gone, the grove slowly trickled back to life. Wind rushed through their hair as they took in the scenery. Fallon wanted to touch Victoria so badly, to pull her close and shower her with affection. She stood deathly still and waited. For Victoria to move first, for her to say something—anything.

She didn't have to wait long.

Victoria quickly closed the distance between them, wrapping her arms around Fallon's neck and burying her face in her hair. "Thank you for pushing me," she said.

Fallon pulled back and braced her arms on Victoria's shoulders. "I am the air beneath your wings, dove. There is no purpose for me without you." She couldn't help it; her eyes briefly shifted to Victoria's trembling lips before she could stop herself. "Did I say something wrong? Why are you crying?" Her hand moved to the nape of Victoria's neck.

"No! No, you didn't say anything wrong," Victoria wiped under her teary eyes. "You've been nothing but supportive and understanding and patient with me." She shook her head softly, wondering how she had became so lucky.

"There was never another option for me, Vic. It's always been you."

Victoria let out a laugh while tears brimmed in her eyes. Her hands rested on either side of Fallon's face as her eyes traced every feature. "I love you." She couldn't speak louder than a whisper, worried her voice would break. She wanted Fallon to hear her clearly—to know she meant it.

Fallon let out a sob before covering her mouth with her hand. "I would fall a million times for you, Victoria." She pulled her by her arms until they were flushed against one another and kissed the side of her head. "I love you too," she said quietly.

The Sun began to set, rich colors enveloping the grove in warm shades of pink and orange.

Fallon pulled back to view the color-drenched field. "Vic," she said. "Look at the sky."

Victoria lifted her head and wiped the tears from her cheeks. She turned from Fallon and stepped away as if she could get closer to the sky. "Do you think..."

Fallon came up behind her and rested her chin on Victoria's shoulder. "Yeah, Vic. I think so."

The two of them sat cross-legged in the center of the field, their fingers intertwined.

"I can't believe that actually worked," Victoria confessed. "For a moment there, I truly expected it to fail..."

Fallon gripped her chin between her fingers and turned her face. "I didn't." When Victoria dipped her head in doubt, she continued. "You're the most capable person I know, Vic. I had full confidence that even if it didn't work that time, you would keep going until you figured it out. I would never doubt you."

Victoria let those words settle in her chest. "Thank you, Fallon." She leaned in and placed a soft kiss against her flushed cheek before leaning into her side. "Well, what do we do now?"

Fallon thought about it. She stared at the vibrant clouds and read them as a sign of a brighter future, filled with life and learning for both of them. "Whatever it is," she moved a piece of Victoria's hair behind her shoulder, "we'll do it together."

Epilogue

Fallon's arms ached from how full the basket was. Fruits from their harvest fell over each other onto the ground, only to be picked up by Victoria.

"Need some help, love?"

Fallon scrambled, trying to deny it, but eventually sighed. "I suppose I do," she admitted.

Victoria placed the dropped fruits in the crook of her arm and looped the other through Fallon's, careful not to disturb the over-filled basket. "Look who's getting better at asking for help," she cheered. "Only took..." She began counting on her fingers.

Fallon howled with laughter, almost sending the entire basket to the ground. "I don't need to be reminded of my centuries of stubbornness, dove. Old habits die hard."

They arrived at the cottage, soft music spilling from inside. Victoria pushed the door open with her foot, allowing Fallon to step in first. "You wash, I'll peel?"

Fallon set their bounty on the counter with a thud, collecting the fruits that spilled over when she did. "That sounds good to me." She leaned in to place a kiss on Victoria's cheek, who turned at the last moment. She smiled against Victoria's lips, her hands falling to her waist. Victoria smiled so wide at her maneuver that Fallon was practically kissing her teeth. After a tender moment of hands in hair and soft moans, they pulled apart. Fallon's eyes traced every line on Victoria's face, lingering around the corners of her eyes and her cupid's bow.

"What's going on up here?" Victoria asked, softly tapping Fallon's temple before tucking a strand of hair behind her ear.

Fallon sighed, her chest heavy with emotion. "I'm the luckiest person in the world."

Victoria scoffed, smiling as she tried to turn away, but Fallon's grip was tight.

"I mean it," she said. She placed a soft, delicate kiss on Victoria's forehead, her hands resting on either side of her neck. "I've existed for centuries," she pointed out. "Nothing has ever made me as happy as you do."

Victoria's heart squeezed in her chest. "Always the romantic," she whispered, her voice breaking.

When they finally came down from their emotional high, they readied the picked fruit for preservation. Fallon used their garden to make the baked goods she sold in town, and Victoria had turned to making jam after Emil's passing. True to his word, Fallon had a home with him. They watched as time stole from him his strength and mobility until, one morning, he didn't wake. They knew it would happen; he had warned them and made them promise not to let his farm crumble after his return to the ground, which is where he requested his final resting place to be.

During Victoria's transition into human life, they spent many long afternoons and evenings lying in the field as a family. Fallon still ached from his absence; it had been almost a year since they buried him in the grove, and their closest friends gathered to celebrate the man that was Emil Nielson. Each one shared a happy or funny memory about the closest person Fallon had to a father before saying their final goodbyes. A stone slab marked his position in the earth, now surrounded by greenery planted by Victoria.

Fallon's dove orchid flourished in the gentle surroundings of the meadow so much so that Fern gifted her the other.

"You took better care of it than I ever did," she confessed. "What's your secret?"

Fallon and Victoria looked at each other and giggled. "Years of practice."

Fern smiled at them in disbelief with raised brows. "You both look younger than me, and you're putting me to shame." She put a hand beside her mouth, hiding her words from the other customers. "Don't tell anybody, alright? I've got a business to run, here."

As the sun set through the window, they settled onto the couch. Fallon's arm rested around Victoria's shoulder as she cuddled into her side, and the DVD player whirred past the title screen. It wasn't long after dark that Victoria fell asleep in Fallon's arms. Fallon had no plans to move, content with being trapped on the couch by the woman she loved. In the light of flickering candles, she looked around their living room.

They didn't change much after Emil passed; he had surprisingly good taste in home decor. They added bits of personal effects, but didn't alter anything of note. New photos adorned the wall in simple wooden frames, some of them taken by Fallon of Victoria in the garden, others of Emil and Fallon in front of a birthday cake that she had made for him in his later years, tiny paper hats on their heads with strings around their chins. Her personal favorite, Fallon thought, was the one of her holding a single fish. Her disgusted face looked over at the slippery creature she held onto with a pair of pliers, and the jeans around her hips gaped on all sides.

"You're putting me on the wall?"

"Of course you're going on the wall. We never got to have kids of our own, but...I think August would've really liked you."

Fallon felt peace knowing they were finally together again. Although she didn't know where they ended up, still unpacking everything she knew about the afterlife, something in her knew that they had found each other. She still wore Emil's clothes. The sleeves of his flannels were far too long, but she didn't care. She rolled them 3-4 times and pulled them tight when she needed a moment with him.

As she looked down at Victoria's sleeping face, her lips parted slightly, and she breathed deeply.

After everything, she thought, it had all been worth it.

Acknowledgements

Fall from Grace pulled more tears from me than I ever thought possible. I spent countless coffee shop writing days crying into my latte as I wrote about these girls, and it didn't get better when reading it all back.

In the face of the world, they settled something in me. Throughout the entire process of the this book, they felt so *real* to me. And I slowly began to realize, it's because they *are*. The story of growing up in the church, only to unlearn all the harmful teachings and rhetoric? It's not an uncommon story, and it's one I know a lot of my readers will share. Growing up queer is incredibly scary, especially when you're surrounded by people you know and love and trust telling you how *wrong* it all is.

There is nothing wrong with being lesbian, gay, trans, non-binary, bisexual, or any other label that falls under the scope of *queer*. The administration is the USA would have you believe otherwise.

Do not let them break you.

As a child, Audrey received an award for *Best Storyteller*.
Little did her elementary teacher know that it would stay
with her forever.

She was raised in Florida, spent far too long in Texas, and
now resides in South Carolina with her husband and their
two pets. Her stories are filled with fantasy and banter, with
relatable characters and real struggles.

She is an avid Renaissance faire attendee who enjoys
weightlifting and Dungeons and Dragons. A theater kid in
every sense of the word, she fills her life with whimsy in every
way she can.